JUBAL STONE: U.S. MARSHAL

TWISTED JUSTICE

CASEY NASH

PRODUCTIONS

INTRODUCTION

A dozen angry men came boiling over the rise riding fast horses and firing their weapons at the settler families as they danced to celebrate the building of the Bly's large two-story barn. The marauders wore flour sacks over their heads with holes for their eyes and mouths. Fiddles and accordions blared joyful tunes across the Kansas Plains but were quickly drowned out by the deluge of gunfire, screams, and yes... laughter, eerie laughter coming from the mouths of the riders.

A haze of grayish-black burnt gunpowder floated in the air like a thick, slow-moving storm cloud. The acrid smell of the smoke caused some to cough; others rubbed their eyes of the irritant as they scattered in the panic, a testament to the plethora of guns that had been fired.

Children were crying. Women were wailing, and blood was staining the ground. The men among the settlers were the obvious intended targets of the assassins. The mission of the armed intruders was to eliminate them all. The slaughter was gruesome. And all because one man, a cattle baron who owned the largest spread in the territory, wanted—no, demanded—more acres for ranch expansion. Twenty thousand acres was just not enough.

As the surviving settlers ran for cover, two of the horsemen lit cloth-wrapped torches soaked in kerosene. Through loud, angry demands to vacate the property, they rode wildly toward the newly constructed barn. One of the Bly's neighbors who was present ran for his wagon and grabbed up his shotgun. Before he could point it toward one of the assassins, his actions were quickly met with deadly force, two slugs from a Winchester at less than twenty yards.

With the barn now fully engulfed in flames, the arsonists lit more torches and turned their attention to the Blys' residence. Mary Bly ran for the house, pleading for them to stop. She was knocked down by one of the riders. He shoved a boot into her back, which sent her headlong to the ground. Then he wheeled his horse and trampled her under the hooves of the big black that the rider gigged unmercifully with his spurs.

An hour later, the only thing left of the Blys' homestead was smoking nails and cinders along with many dead bodies, including one of the Blys' children, Delbert, a two-week-old boy who was in the front room of the cabin asleep when it was torched.

Eutychus Bly watched in horror from underneath a wagon. He was only a child then, around six years old, but the events of that fateful day had haunted him all his life. Eutychus would never forget seeing his mother crawl toward the burning house screaming Delbert's name. Mentally, his ma would never be the same. She seemed to do a lot of staring up into the sky and wiping tears from her eyes in the years that followed. Physically, she walked with a noticeable limp the rest of her life.

Had that been the only time landgrabbers victimized his family, it would have been one too many times. However, this happened again, twice, after Eutychus himself married and had children of his own.

This peace-loving man, a man who believed what his parents taught him that there was good in everyone, a man who lived by the philosophy to live and let live, reached his breaking point. He was now ready to trade his plow in for a rifle.

Eutychus Bly would now take up the cause of the underdog, the unrepresented, the put-upon, the settler families who only wanted a better life and the liberty to live it but were denied it. His mission to rid Kansas and the rest of the frontier of land-grabbers, greedy cattle barons, and other men set on taking from others what didn't belong to them, would later make Bly a hero and crusader of what many would come to call 'twisted justice.'

1

"I'll be back directly," said Myra as she picked up the reins of the team and clucked. She had just dropped Eutychus and their son, Del, off by the creek. The father and son boasted of how they'd have supper caught up lickety-split and would need a wagon to tote their catch.

Amused by their boasting, Myra smiled and shook her head as she turned the horses toward the Blounts' homestead where she planned to barter a smoked ham for some of Karen Blount's fresh eggs and cheese.

Del wasted no time getting to the creek bank, to the deep, jade green hole of water where he had caught fish before. Grabbing up the hook, he ran the sharp barb the length of the worm, then dropped his line in the water with great anticipation. Instantly, he hooked a two-pound catfish. Del could hardly compose himself.

"I got one, Pa! I got one!" he yelled as he tugged on the willow pole, man against fish.

Eutychus was standing on a flat rock about to toss in his line when he turned and saw his son hauling in the fish. Smiling with great satisfaction, he said, "Well, you rascal. You didn't even give me a chance to—"

Before he could finish what he was saying, his head jerked toward the homestead. He smelled smoke. His heart missed a beat, fearing the worst. Fire was a great threat on the Plains. It was a thief among the settlers. It had robbed many of their homes, barns, crops, and sometimes their lives.

Dropping his pole on the big rock he was standing on, he ordered Del to come with him. Del didn't say a word. He just laid his pole down beside the flailing fish he had just caught and tried his best to keep up with his pa. They ran as fast as they could for home.

Reaching the rise overlooking their homestead, they were both out of breath as they looked down in horror and saw a plume of smoke coming from their house. The wheat field was also on fire and the Kansas wind was spreading it faster than gangrene in a neglected wound. In less than five minutes, twenty acres of prime wheat, just days away from harvesting, disappeared in the flames. Black ashes covered the dirt. That's all that was left. Everything Eutychus and his family had worked for the last year since purchasing the homestead was now up in smoke.

"Pa, what are we going to do? Our wheat crop is gone," asked the twelve-year-old Del as he fought back tears, his voice cracking. He didn't want to cry in front of his pa, but even as young as he was, he seemed to understand that his and his family's survival depended on the wheat crop that was now laying in ashes.

Eutychus pulled his son to his side and consoled him the

best he could. Then, with a stern stare, he looked across the homestead and wondered what had happened. If it was what he thought it was, he had already decided it was time to take a different tack.

By the time Eutychus and Del got back to the house, it was fully engulfed. There was nothing they could do besides watch in horror from the entrance of the barn. Somehow, the barn was untouched, even though it was only thirty yards from the house. Eutychus didn't understand how it was still standing, but at the moment was glad that at least he and his family would have a roof over their heads that night.

About an hour later, Myra stopped at the creek bank to pick up Eutychus and Del. She had made a good trade with Mrs. Blount and even enjoyed some tea with her. But as she searched the creek bank for her husband and son, they were nowhere to be found. She yelled their names but got no answer.

Climbing down out of the buggy she stepped over to where she last saw them standing and saw one of the willow poles they used for fishing. It was laying alongside the creek bank. Then she saw the catfish Del had caught lying stiff and dried out beside the pole. Myra knew neither Eutychus nor Del would treat a fish like that, especially one they planned to eat. Her hand went to her chest as she frantically stared up and down the creek.

Running toward the wagon, she climbed aboard and raced toward home. She smelled fire in the air as she got closer. Then she saw the charred wheat field. She gasped and closed her eyes. Then she turned the team toward the house and whipped them into a run. As she got closer, she saw the house, or what was left of it, laying in charred ruins.

Eutychus, Del!" she screamed as she pulled the team to a stop. They hurried out of the barn to meet her.

"Oh, Eutychus. What happened?"

Eutychus stared at her for a few moments before he answered. Then he looked off to the west of the homestead and said with an eerie calmness, "Herman Stokes."

"How do you know that, Eutychus? I mean, couldn't a spark from the stove pipe have started the fire in the house and spread to the field?"

Eutychus shook his head and bent his thumb toward the barn.

"Fire didn't shoot the milk cow or kill all the hogs," he said flatly. The horrors of what happened to him in the past at the hands of evil men were flooding his mind. Today marked the turning point for Eutychus Bly. He could no longer turn a deaf ear, a blind eye, or a cheek to the atrocities that had happened to him and his family.

A peaceful man he had been all his life, a man who would give you the shirt off his back, the last cup of his coffee, and the last spoonful of his beans. But he'd had enough, and soon those who ran rough-shod over the innocent were going to be paid the wages of their sins.

Myra felt a chill go down her spine. Never in their marriage had she seen her husband like this. It was as if he had become another man since she dropped him off at the creek. However, that wasn't all that was plaguing her right now. She cupped her mouth with a hand as her eyes wandered off to the left. The wheat field was charred black. In the background were three riders on the rise, watching.

Del climbed up in the wagon and hugged his ma. Then he said, "Pa said it's time for us to take a different tack."

4

Myra wiped the tears from her cheeks and asked with trepidation, "What do you mean by that, Eutychus?"

He did not respond, not with words anyway. He walked straight to the barn and took an axe out of the tool room. Then he walked toward the wagon. Even the way he moved seemed strange to Myra. His steps were wooden-like and his face was that of granite as he laid the axe on the floor of the wagon.

Myra climbed down and stepped in front of him. "What are doing, Eutychus?

He was totally despondent, except to put his boot on the wheel and climb aboard.

"Where are you going, Eutychus?" she asked again with raised palms as she stared up to man who seemed to be in another world.

Again, he didn't answer. He just released the brake, raised the reins, and slapped them against the rumps of the horses. They galloped forward as Myra closed her eyes and buried her face in her hands. She feared the next time she saw Eutychus it would be with a blanket laid over his body.

2

As Eutychus got closer to Herman Stokes' ranch, three riders intercepted him, the same ones who were perched on the hill earlier.

"Where you headed, Bly?" one of them asked as one of his hands rested atop the saddle horn with the reins laced between his fingers. His other hand messaged the grip of his Colt.

Eutychus' head didn't move, but his eyes did. He looked dead at the man and said, "To get reimbursed for my losses or kill Herman Stokes. His choice."

He raised the reins and snapped them like a whip. As he moved forward, instantly he felt the sting of a rope tightening around his neck, then another fell over his shoulders. The two men yanked Eutychus from the wagon seat then stepped down and gave him a beating.

As he lay on the ground with his face down in some sage, Stokes' men kicked him. Then they taunted him with words about his wife.

"She ain't much to look at, but I reckon I might just go over and say howdy anyway. What would you think about that, Bly?" one of them chuckled.

Another of the men reached down and slipped his loop off Eutychus' neck and coiled up his rope. Throwing it over his saddle horn, he said, "If I were you, sodbuster, I'd pack up your missus and that young'un of yourn and scat. This part of Kansas doesn't seem to agree with you. Now, Mr. Stokes has been more than fair in his offer to purchase your place, but you and those nesters are a stubborn bunch. It's a pity your house and wheat burned, but next time, you won't live to grieve the loss."

Suddenly the men heard riders coming. When they turned around, they saw Herman Stokes and two more of his hired guns.

"We were just teaching Mr. Bly here a lesson, boss." He reached into Eutychus' wagon and pulled the axe off the floor-board below the seat. "Looks like Mr. Bly intended you harm. Told us that you'd either reimburse him for his losses or he would take your life." The man rubbed his fingers over the axe. "Sharp."

"Throw his carcass in the wagon and send that team on its way." Stokes rode up next to Eutychus and pointed down. "The next time you ride across my property, it will be your last time. You'd be wise to fold up your tent and move on, Bly. I've had a bait of you nesters scarring the land with your plows."

Stokes stood in his stirrups and surveilled the landscape. With a wave of a finger, he said, "This here is cattle country. In the next few years, I plan to own every homestead and acre you and the other trespassers are sitting on. Going to make a name for myself, a name that will be remembered across Kansas." He spat and motioned with his head for his men to load Bly into his wagon and send him on his way.

3

Jubal walked into the judge's office and tipped his hat to Edna Creel, his secretary. "Good morning, Mrs. Creel. I heard the judge wanted to see me."

"Yes, Marshal Stone. He told me to let him know when you arrived. I'll see if he's available." She pointed to the coffee pot. "Help yourself to the coffee. I just made a fresh pot."

"Obliged. I believe I will," he said as he lifted his hat and hung it on the hat rack by the door.

"Jubal," he heard the judge say down the hall. "Come on in."

Stone hurried to pour himself a cup of coffee then turned sideways so he and Mrs. Creel could pass in the hallway.

"Morning, Judge."

"And good afternoon to you," Brewster snarled. He looked at his wall clock and said, "You took your sweet time gettin' here. And I bet you didn't even bring me a cup of coffee."

"But I did, Judge," said Edna as she tapped on his door.

"Bless you, Edna."

"Yes, Mrs. Edna, bless you. Looks like the judge is on the prod this morning. Maybe a cup of that will settle him down."

Brewster tossed Jubal a stern look and said, "Don't count on it, Marshal."

Jubal smiled then winked at Edna as he took a sip of his coffee.

"Is there anything else I can get for you, Judge?" asked Mrs. Creel as she took hold of the doorknob to close the door.

"No, that will be all, Edna. Thank you."

As she closed the door, Leon pointed to a chair. "Take a seat, Jubal. Like I said, you took your time gettin' over here, so let's get down to business."

Jubal raised a hand. "Now, Judge, let me explain. When F.M. gave me your message, I was right in the middle of settling a dispute."

"Yeah. Who's got their hackles up now?"

"You mean besides you?" Jubal chuckled.

Leon remained straight-faced as he reached into his shirt pocket for a cigar.

Jubal moved to the edge of his chair and said, "Hank and Ed Wright were at it again down at the livery. About to pull guns on each other, they were."

"What'd you do with them?"

"Threw them both in jail to cool off."

"Good. I've told those two myself what I'd do to them if they locked horns again."

"Now, what is it, Judge, that you wanted to see me about?"

"Besides a stack of warrants that need to be served, I got me a quite interesting letter from the governor of Kansas, Bill Hoppe."

"Well, Judge, as for those warrants..."

"Forget about those right now, Jubal," Brewster held up a hand. "Read this," he said as he took the letter off his desk and leaned over toward Jubal. "See if that won't blow your boots off your feet." The judge lit up his cigar and watched Jubal's reaction as he read the governor's request.

Jubal suddenly stopped reading and looked up at Brewster. Raising the letter in the air and pointing to it, he said, "Is Governor Hoppe on the level? I mean..."

Brewster took a long drag of his cigar and blew the smoke upward. Then he chuckled. "I believe he is. What do you say? Would you be willing to do what he's asking?"

Jubal pointed down at the stack of warrants.

"I don't see how I could take on another chore, Judge, with all these warrants that need to be served."

Leon waved a dismissive hand and pursed his lips. "F.M. and Curly can handle those. Back to the governor's request, what do you say?"

Curly, the blacksmith, served as a deputy marshal when he was needed. He was a bit sweet on F.M. Miller. He stayed deputized in case Jubal needed him in a hurry. And because Tanner Burns was still in Burnett serving temporarily as the town's lawman, the need to call on Curly could become a reality quickly.

Jubal, as often he did when faced with a challenge or was agitated, rubbed the back of his neck as he stared at the judge. "Is this an order from you, Judge, or do I have choice in the matter?"

Leon quickly removed his cigar from his mouth and pointed at the marshal. "Dang it, Jubal, you know you have a choice. Have I ever ordered you to do anything?"

"Well—"

Before Stone could finish his answer, the judge said, "All right, maybe I have once or twice, but not this time. You decide what you're going to do, and I'll let Governor Hoppe know you're answer."

Jubal stared back down at the letter and studied it a bit more. Putting his finger to the paper, he said, "Special Range Detective. What do you know about that, Judge? And who is this Eutychus Bly?"

"All I know is Kansas, like Texas, has its share of greedy men who want to own the whole state and they'll kill to get it. And like Texas, Kansas doesn't have enough lawmen to be everywhere at one time to stop them."

"And Eutychus Bly?"

"I know very little about him. Governor Hoppe said he wants to send him and two others our way so you can teach them everything a frontier lawman needs to know about the law, about guns, and about how to stay alive when others are trying to kill you."

"But why me, Judge? There's plenty of Kansas lawmen who could do that."

"The governor wants this to be kept under our hats. This special range detective is going to go undercover. He'll have a badge and the authority to enforce Kansas law, but no one will know that but us."

With slight agitation, Jubal rubbed his ear and said, "When would you like for me to begin the training?"

The judge was sitting on the edge of his desk when he rose up and said with excitement, "So you're willing to work with these men, Jubal?"

"Yes, sir. If that's what you'd have me do."

Leon slapped his leg and said, "Splendid. I'll send a wire

today telling the governor of our conversation. Then we'll wait to hear back from him." Brewster looked down at the stack of warrants and pointed. "In the meantime, try to get as many of these served as you can."

Jubal took a big swallow of his coffee and said, "I'll expect some of this Arbuckle's out of this."

"I'll have Mrs. Creel bring you some, and how's that bottle of rye holding up?"

"About empty."

"Another one's on the way."

"All right, Judge." Jubal smiled as he stood to his feet. Reaching down, he picked up the warrants. "Reckon I better rattle my hocks before my new duties begin: training special range detectives."

Leon smiled and walked toward the door with Jubal. "You and Nancy are still coming to dinner tomorrow night, right?"

"Yes, sir."

Leon pointed. "You be sure to bring little Monty now. I haven't seen my buddy this week. Bet he's growing like a weed."

"That he is, Judge. That he is."

The next evening, Jubal and his family enjoyed a nice meal with the Brewsters. They had roasted Cornish hens, scalloped potatoes, and creamed corn. For dessert, Lucy baked a fresh apple pie.

Nancy enjoyed the delicious meal for a couple of reasons. One was because Lucy held Monty during the whole supper, giving Nancy a needed break and time to eat. And second, because the Cornish hens were a rarity.

Jubal enjoyed his meal as well. When he polished off his big piece of apple pie, he wiped his mouth with the cloth in his lap and sat back.

"Mrs. Lucy, that was fine vittles."

"It certainly was. I haven't had Cornish hens since I was a little girl. It was very good," smiled Nancy.

Jubal's eyes narrowed as he looked across the table at Leon.

"I figure you heard from the governor, Judge. Is that what this big fine meal is about?"

Leon pulled a cigar from his vest and leaned over to the lantern and held it there until the stogie glowed red at the end.

"Now, Marshal Stone," he said in light rebuke, "are you accusing a federal judge of trying to win the favor of a marshal?"

Lucy bounced Monty on her knee and frowned. "And just what are you two up to? Nancy, what are we going to do with them?"

"I don't know, Mrs. Lucy. But they do look like they are up to something. You gentlemen care to let us in on it?"

"Judge," said Jubal, "I figure since this is your catfish you ought to skin it."

Lucy stared at Leon. "Judge, what do you have up your sleeve?"

Leon puffed on his cigar and looked up to the ceiling. Then he looked down at Monty.

"Why can't you womenfolk be like Monty there? You don't hear him asking any questions, now, do you?"

Monty smiled as Leon looked at him. The judge pointed. "Did you see that? I told you that boy liked me."

"He sure does, Judge," said Jubal. "He talks about you all the time."

Nancy tapped Jubal on the arm and pursed her lips. "Jubal."

"Well, doesn't he, honey? Judge Brewster, that's all I hear from Monty these days," Jubal continued prodding the judge.

Leon shook his head and stuck his stogie back in his mouth. Then he winked at Monty.

Jubal and Nancy appreciated the connection they had with the Brewsters and how much Lucy and Leon loved their son, Monty.

"So, Mrs. Lucy and I are not going to hear about what you two have cooking?" asked Nancy.

Jubal threw up both hands. "I don't have anything cooking. This is the judge's pot of soup."

"Leon, I think it's time you spilled the beans. You know I'll get it out of you one way or another," warned Lucy.

Leon rubbed the top of his head and frowned. "Yeah, I remember the last time when you took that frying pan to my head." He pointed at Lucy as he looked to Nancy. "You wouldn't believe that sweet, little ol' Lucy would do that now would you, Mrs. Stone?"

"What do you mean, old Lucy?"

"I said *ol'*, honey, not *old*."

Everyone laughed then Lucy stared at Leon with her pretty brown eyes and blinked her long eyelashes. "All right, honey."

Leon yanked his cigar from his mouth and held up his hands. "All right. So much for keeping things under wraps, *Marshal Stone*. Governor Hoppe of Kansas wants Jubal to train a special group of lawmen, range detectives I believe he called them." The judge looked across the table and pointed. "You were right about me hearing from him. They should be arriving two days from today."

"Who?" asked Lucy

"The three that Jubal will be training."

"Do you know their names, Judge?" asked Jubal. "Don't reckon any of them are highbinders or bank robbers. Reckon the governor checked them out before sending them our way."

"If I know Bill Hoppe, he's done his homework. His reputation is on the line. You know he's up for reelection this year?"

"No, sir, I didn't know that," Jubal answered. Stone never liked politics and the reelection of a governor in another state really didn't interest him. However, because Judge Brewster seemed to show an interest, he did as well.

Monty began to cry. He was still breastfeeding, and it had been an hour since he had last nursed. Nancy looked over at Jubal and said, "We don't want to wear out our welcome, honey, and I need to nurse Monty Joseph."

"Monty Joseph," said Lucy as she cradled him in her arms. "I sure like that name. The namesake of two great men, Monty Peel and Joe Stone."

Jubal and Nancy smiled at one another, both appreciating and agreeing with what she had just said. Then Jubal stood up and pulled back Nancy's chair. Stepping around the table, he took Monty from Lucy and they all walked to the door.

Helping Nancy up into the buckboard with one hand, Jubal held Monty in the other. Then he passed him off to her. Untying the bay, he climbed in beside Nancy and they were off.

Two days later, the trainees did arrive in Waco, but it wasn't three men.

Judge Brewster and Jubal greeted the Blys as they stepped off the train. It was half past five in the afternoon.

"Eutychus Bly is my name. This is Myra, my wife, and Del, my son. He's named after my brother Delmer." Eutychus held out his hand. Leon and Jubal each shook his hand and introduced themselves.

Jubal readily noticed the bruises on Eutychus' face. He also noticed him favoring his ribs. It looked like he'd been in a fight and lost badly. Stone's guess was spot-on, as he would learn later.

The three Blys stood there on the boardwalk staring up the street of Waco as if they'd never seen a town before. It was obvious to anyone looking that these folks were sodbusters or hicks, as some would call them.

Jubal hid a grin with his hand to his chin and thought, *These folks are green as the water down by Jade Creek.* He glanced over to Leon who looked to be thinking the same thing as the judge studied their faces incredulously.

Jubal and the judge were surprised that Mr. Bly brought his family along. As far as looking inconspicuous and keeping his mission hidden, the Kansan didn't help himself by bringing his wife and kid. But the biggest surprise still awaited Stone and Brewster.

Marshal Stone continued staring toward the unloading passengers, looking for the other two men, as did Brewster. When the conductor stepped off the train, which was a signal there were no more passengers aboard, they looked at one another suspiciously then to the Blys.

Whispering, Brewster said, "Well, Governor Hoppe said he was sending three to Waco. I reckon that's them."

"Wait a minute, Judge. I—"

Jubal's words were interrupted by Eutychus. "Is there a place that my family and I could get a bite to eat? We haven't et since breakfast."

"Why, certainly," answered Brewster as he pointed. "There's

a diner just up the way here. Jubal, let's take them over to Dal's for supper. Then we'll get them settled in at the hotel."

Not wanting to be impolite, Jubal nodded and led the way.

Eutychus picked up his pace and walked beside the marshal. "We sure are obliged that you would take us under your wing, Marshal, and teach us what we need to know."

Jubal glanced over his shoulder and frowned at the judge. But then he saw Myra staring at him and smiling. Turning back to Eutychus, he said, "Glad to help you anyway I can, Mr. Bly."

"Marshal Jubal Stone," came an angry voice from the saloon stoop across the street. There were two men finishing off their beers, one leaning against a post, the other with his boot in one of the chairs.

Jubal threw out a hand to stop Eutychus. "Judge, get them out of the way."

"Come with me, folks," ordered Brewster.

Eutychus looked at Jubal then to the two men and back at Jubal. "Marshal, what can I do to help you?"

Jubal flatly said, "Get out of the way, Bly. Lead is liable to be coming this way."

Eutychus clutched his ribs and limped toward Myra, the judge, and Del as all four of them distanced themselves from Jubal.

"Judge, there's two and the marshal is only one. Shouldn't we try to help him?"

Leon was impressed with Eutychus' courage and was a bit amused at his words. He whispered, "Bly, the best thing we can do for Jubal is stay out of his way. He knows how to handle scum like that."

Brewster looked at Myra and Del and saw horror on their faces. He reached and patted Myra's shoulder and winked at

Del. "It's going to be all right, ma'am. You two get a little closer to this wall over here. Wouldn't want you to catch a stray bullet."

Myra quickly did as Leon said and pulled Del to her. Eutychus stared at the gunmen, wondering what they wanted.

"Here to kill you, Marshal. Me and Everett."

Jubal quickly glanced over his shoulder, making sure there was no one behind him. Then he stared toward the rooftop. Eutychus watched his every move. Then Jubal widened his stance and said, "Is there a reason for that, Riggs?"

"You know who I am, then, Marshal?" he asked with pride and he stuffed his thumbs behind his gun belt. Every gunman wanted his name to be known.

"I know who you are, Riggs, a two-bit gun slick trying to make a name for himself. Who's that other bum with you?"

The man removed his boot from the chair and slammed his empty mug against the wall of the saloon, shattering it into many pieces. Then pointing at Jubal, he said, "I'm the one that's about to take your life, Stone."

Eutychus' head swiveled back and forth, following each man's conversation. Then he took a step forward.

Judge Brewster snapped his fingers and said, "Bly, don't you move another muscle, or you'll draw their fire toward your family."

Eutychus looked back at the judge like an embarrassed child who just got caught with his hand in the cookie jar. He took a step backward, folded his hands down in front of him, and stared down at the boardwalk.

Deputy Marshal F.M. Miller came jogging up the boardwalk. Jubal waved a hand at her and she stopped.

Riggs looked around. Pushing up on the brim of his hat, he

said, "Well, howdy, pretty deputy. When I get finished with your friend yonder, how about you and me getting better acquainted?"

Surprisingly, F.M. answered, "It's a deal, Riggs... but only if you'll stand and brace him alone."

Riggs took the bait. He hollered to his partner, "You heard her, Everett. The marshal's mine."

"What if you can't take him, Riggs?"

Riggs chuckled. "Ain't a man ever survived a gunfight with me. But... if he takes me, then he's yours. But if I take him, the girl is mine."

Jubal took another step closer then dropped his hand to his side. "You're under arrest, Riggs, for murder. Got a poster on you last week. And you, dogface, drop your gun and throw up your hands. Haven't seen your ugly mug on a poster, but that don't mean you're not wanted."

Everett dropped his hand to his gun. Riggs waved a hand in rebuke. "He's mine, Wells. Don't you go drawing on him, or you'll have to deal with me."

Wells reluctantly acquiesced, but Jubal could tell the man was just a second away from boiling over. Jubal Stone was a master at goading gunfighters.

"You look like a little boy, Wells. Like somebody just took away your marbles."

Wells went for his gun, but Jubal's Colt leaped out of leather and was cocked and pointed before Wells could clear leather. Consequently, Everett released his pistol, which fell back into the holster and held up his hands.

"Ease that shooter out of the holster and drop it on the ground."

He did as he was told.

"Now, step back, pup, until I tell you to stop."

Miller had stepped off the boardwalk and was now just a few feet from Wells.

"Keep moving backwards," ordered Jubal.

He did until he felt the hard barrel of Miller's Colt slam the back of his head. His knees buckled, and he fell face down on the ground.

Eutychus looked back at Myra and shook his head. He'd never seen anything like what he was witnessing. He was a farmer, a man of peace, a man who knew little about settling things with a gun, but he knew in this moment he had a lot to learn and was willing to do so.

Riggs was angry that Wells has stolen his show. Raising his finger, he warned Jubal, "Wells was a fool. Slow as molasses in January."

"Not like you, huh?"

"That's right, Stone. I'm going to kill you. Then"—he jabbed his chest—"I'll be the fastest gun on the frontier."

"The biggest fool, you mean."

"Talk is over, Marshal." Riggs' hand quivered with nerves. "I'm going to let my Colt do the rest of my talking."

The gunman crouched and went for his pistol. Jubal's quick draw made it look like his opponent was in slow motion. Fire flared from the bore of Stone's Colt as two quick shots left the barrel. The lead ripped through Riggs' body so fast that it seemed the gunman didn't know he was hit. That is until he put his hand to his chest and looked down. Then he fell to the ground, dead.

Jubal walked over to the downed man and picked up his gun. Then he stepped over to Wells who was starting to wake up. F.M. had already stuck his gun in her belt.

"Take him over to the doc's and get him seen about. Then send him on his way."

"You don't want me to lock him up, Jubal?" asked F.M. disapprovingly.

"He's not wanted, but I don't want him in Waco either."

Jubal moved closer and spoke calmly to Wells. "Don't you ever come to Waco again, or I'll kill you. Do you understand?"

Wells grinned but didn't answer.

Jubal slapped him across the face. "I asked you, mister, do you understand?"

"Yes, I understand."

"You came to town today to take my life, and you don't even know me. But I promise you this, if we ever meet again, and you're toting that gun, I won't show you any mercy."

Wells knew Jubal had spared his life. And he also knew that what he had come to Waco to do was against the law. He could have been jailed.

Miller grabbed him by the arm and swung him around. "Let's go, Wells."

Judge Brewster looked at the Blys and said, "You folks stay put." Then he waved a hand toward F.M. and said, "Hold up there, Deputy."

Leon walked briskly toward Jubal and pointed toward Wells. "You aren't going to let that killer off scot-free are you, Marshal? You hadn't forgotten that I'm a judge and can charge him with an attempt on the life of a federal marshal. He'll spend most of the rest of his life behind bars."

F.M. continued holding Wells by the arm as she stared at Jubal for instruction. Jubal gestured for her to carry on, which she did. Then he looked at Brewster and said, "Maybe he's learned his lesson, Judge."

"Yeah," protested Leon, "and maybe he hasn't. I say he needs about twenty years in jail to think about what he came here to do."

Jubal smiled at Brewster and leaned in. Whispering, he said, "I think you've made your point, Judge. Just look at Wells staring down at the ground."

Leon winked then straightened. "All right, Marshal. At your request, I'll let this man go." He pointed to Wells. "But if I had my way, young man, you'd be in hand irons and riding that prison wagon that leaves out of here each week."

Wells looked at Miller, hoping she was ready to fetch him to the doc. Then he planned to ride hard and fast away from Waco. At the moment, he had no plans to return, ever.

4

As Jubal and Brewster walked back toward the Blys, they could tell Myra and Del were shaken by the experience. Eutychus, on the other hand, was full of questions.

"Marshal, I wanted to help you, but didn't know what to do."

Brewster chuckled. "Dang if I don't think Eutychus was going to tie into them with his bare knuckles. I had to keep a tight rein on him from over there."

"Obliged, Eutychus, for wanting to help," said Jubal as he pulled his Colt and replaced the spent cartridges with fresh rounds, "but you need to learn to control your emotions when dealing with that kind." He threw a thumb over his shoulder back to where Riggs lay. A blanket was already being spread to cover his body.

Del stared at Jubal as he replaced the bullets and spun his pistol back into leather. Jubal was not doing that for show; it's just how he normally holstered his gun after using it.

Wow, thought Del. *I wonder if Pa will ever be able to do that? Shucks, maybe I can even learn.*

Myra sighed deeply. She had not taken the experience as well as Eutychus and Del. But she knew going back to Kansas without knowing how to defend herself and her family was not an option. When the landgrabbers burned their house and wheat field, something changed in her and Eutychus. They vowed never to be at the mercy of the enemy again. Thus, they were bound and determined to learn the skills needed to protect themselves as well as others who dreamed of having their own land without fear of it being violently and illegally stripped of them.

"Ma'am," said Jubal as he removed his hat, "are you all right?"

"Yes, Marshal Stone, I am. But I sure would like to sit a spell. I'm feeling a bit weak."

Eutychus stepped up next to his wife and took her by the arm. "Come on, Myra. Let's get something to eat. She tends to get weak when she hasn't eaten."

Jubal and Judge Brewster followed behind them, discussing what had just happened.

"Did you know that Riggs was in the area, Jubal?"

"Yes, sir, I did. Got a wire from the constable out of Rusk saying he had been spotted."

Brewster shook his head and continued to speak softly. Motioning with his head to the Blys, he said, "I regret they had to see that, being fresh to town and all."

Jubal's bottom lip protruded. "Might be good that they did, Judge. I wouldn't have been able to explain to Eutychus some of what I've got to teach him if he didn't see the need for it. If he's going to be a range detective on the frontier, he's got to expect to run up against the likes of Riggs."

"I suppose you're right."

Jubal pulled on his ear and smiled. "What was that you said, Judge?"

"I said, I suppose you're right."

Jubal chuckled. "That's what I thought you said. I just don't hear you say it too often."

"That's because—"

"I know, Judge," Jubal said with a hand in the air. "It's because I'm seldom right. Right?"

"Correct," grinned Leon as they were now just a few feet from the diner stoop.

"Hold up there, Eutychus," said Jubal. Jubal glanced toward Brewster. "How are we going to introduce the Blys, Judge?"

Leon raised his derby and scratched his head. "Well—"

"Judge," interrupted Eutychus. "Governor Hoppe's got that figured out. It's here in this letter."

Jubal and Leon stared at one another, wondering why they had not received this information beforehand. Leon took the letter from Eutychus and perused it quickly.

"That rascal," snarled Brewster.

"What, Judge?" asked Jubal as they stood just a few feet from the doorway of the diner.

"Take a gander at that." He pushed the letter toward Jubal and tucked his fingers into his vest pockets.

"He knew all along, didn't he, Judge?" said Jubal.

Eutychus sensed the men were feeling put upon. "Excuse me, Judge Brewster and Marshal Stone. Sounds like our coming here was on pretense. I thought the governor had talked to you two about teaching me the skills of a lawman? If that's not the case, maybe we best pull out of here tomorrow. We wouldn't want to cause you any trouble." He looked back to his wife. "Would we, Myra?"

"No, we certainly wouldn't. It's just that..." She broke down and began to weep.

Eutychus stepped over and pulled her to himself. "It's all right, honey." Del put his arms around his mother's waist to console her.

Jubal looked away, not sure how to react to Myra's emotion. He wished in that moment that Nancy or Mrs. Lucy was there. They would know what to say. But neither was so he thought for a moment. Then suddenly, he looked back to them with a resolute stare. "We'll do as the governor suggested." His head swiveled quickly to Leon. "Judge, how about the Dawsons' place? They won't be back from Missouri until the spring. Until then couldn't Eutychus and his family live there? Hoppe suggested we introduce the Blys as farmers."

Leon snapped his fingers and smiled. "That's a splendid idea. You folks could even work the land if you have a mind to."

Eutychus removed his hat and held it between his hands. Shaking his head, he said sheepishly, "I'm afraid we don't have..."

Brewster patted Eutychus on the shoulder. "Ted Dawson has everything you need there in that barn of his."

Leon pointed to Jubal. "Let's step in here and introduce our newest residents of Waco. Farmers from Kansas that want to try their hand in the Texas soil, shall we?"

Jubal nodded. "Yes, we shall. After you, Mr. and Mrs. Bly and Del." He pulled open the door and stepped aside. The Blys hesitated. "Well, I thought you folks were hungry?" said Jubal.

Myra wiped her tears and smiled. "Bless you, Marshal

Stone, and you too, Judge Brewster." She smiled warmly at both of them and they all went inside.

As they ate supper together, Jubal was amused as he watched young Del devour three biscuits that were laden with thick, white gravy. He thought, *One day Monty will be about Del's size and probably have the same kind of appetite if he's anything like his pa.* Just the thought of that made Jubal want a second helping of mashed potatoes. He didn't want Del feeling like he was eating alone.

Myra wiped her mouth with the cloth napkin then cleared her throat as she clasped her hands together and rested them atop the table. Looking at Judge Brewster, then to Jubal, she said, "Judge, Marshal, I figure I owe you two an explanation for my behavior earlier."

"No, no, you don't, Mrs. Bly," Leon assured her.

Jubal echoed the Leon's sentiments. "No need for that, ma'am."

"You are very kind, but if you would allow me to tell you what brings us here."

Jubal's eyebrows arched as he glanced at Brewster. He wondered if they were now going to get another big surprise.

Myra took a deep breath and looked at her husband then to her son, who was fixated on the apple pie he was about to jab a fork into.

"Eutychus would never tell you what I'm about to tell you, but I think it's necessary to get this said." She looked to the marshal and judge for their permission to continue.

"We're listening, ma'am," said Jubal.

Eutychus stared nervously out one of the windows, knowing what his wife was about to say. He was a quiet man who kept his feelings to himself. That was sometimes part of his problem. But the trauma that had happened over the last twenty years of his life needed to be communicated.

"What would cause a man and his family to pull up stakes and move to another state? To boot, to begin a new profession that my husband knows nothing about: a frontier lawman? On its face, that sounds crazy, but please listen to our story."

Jubal pulled his chair up closer and leaned forward, as did Leon. They didn't want anyone to hear what Myra was about to say. It was none of their business, and it might jeopardize the Blys' mission.

"When Eutychus was six years old, a cattle baron who owned thousands of acres sent twelve riders to the Bly homestead. They killed six men that day, one woman, and a child, Delbert Bly, Eutychus' two-week-old baby brother." Myra stared over at her son. "Del is named after his uncle.

"Eutychus' father, Ezekiel, was a gentle man. He didn't believe in taking up arms against nobody for no reason. He taught his son"—she patted Eutychus on the hand—"that there was good in every person if you looked for it."

Eutychus wiped tears from his eyes as he listened to his wife put into words his life's story. It was painful.

"Those riders burned everything that the Blys had. They crippled his mother as one of them trampled her underfoot of his horse. So, they moved to another part of Kansas and started over. Eutychus here married and had a child. Until one day, landgrabbers showed up and... Well, Eutychus buried his wife and child and moved to Kingman. That's where he and I met. We got married and had Del yonder."

Myra took a deep breath and continued. "One day I was off visiting our neighbors." Myra smiled as she held up her hands. "Had me a big, fine smoked ham that Eutychus had prepared. Going to do some bartering, I was, for some fresh eggs and cheese. The fox had gotten into our coop and killed most of our laying hens. I came back by the creek to pick up Eutychus and Del. They had promised to catch supper and by jingo they were doing a good job of it... until Eutychus smelled smoke.

"Well, when I got to the creek to pick up my men, they weren't there. But I saw that big fish, Del, that you caught. He was a fine one."

Del lit up when his ma said that. He held up his hands to show the size of it. Everybody laughed, including Myra. Del, like most fishermen, embellished a bit.

Myra took another deep breath then continued. "I wheeled for home. When I got there, I saw the house in a pile of smoking rubble and the wheat was charred black from the fire. Thought maybe a spark from the stovepipe had started it until Dell broke the news that someone had shot the cow and all our hogs. He believed it to be Herman Stokes, a man who owned over twenty-five thousand acres, but them acres were just not enough. He wanted ours as well.

"That is why we are here, Marshal Stone and Judge Brewster. My husband and I have just about given up hope. We spent everything we had to buy our homestead. Had us a fine stand of hard red winter wheat. It was less than a week away from harvesting. Then they burned it. Our dreams went up in smoke. We believe the Good Lord gives people a right to live in freedom, to work their lands, and enjoy the fruit of their labor. No man has a right to take that away from them."

When Myra finished, there was complete silence for the next few minutes. Jubal had drunk from the well of sorry himself, losing his parents and sister to assassins, and Judge

Brewster also knew the heartache of losing family as he too had lost his wife to a violent killing.

Suddenly, young Del broke the silence. "That was a mighty big catfish I caught that day. Ma, I still say he was every bit of this long." Again, he held his hands apart, this time even wider than before.

Del's words brought some much-needed levity to the table. Everyone laughed. Then Jubal called for the check. He and Judge Brewster argued over who would pay until Leon pulled rank on him.

"A judge outranks a marshal any day of the week, even on Sundays." His words also brought laughter to the table and a big thank you from the Blys for supper.

As Jubal and Leon got the Blys settled in at the hotel, they walked back to the jail and had a nightcap, a good stiff shot of rye.

"Them poor folks have been down the river and might near hit every rock along the way. But dang, Judge, I don't even know where to start in training them for what's ahead. I was expecting three men and was dreading even that. Now we find out it's a man, his wife, and their twelve-year-old son."

"I've got a mind to send Governor Hoppe a telegram and give him down the country. He knew doggone well what he was doing when he sent them to Waco."

"Yeah, well, when you get finished with him, I'm like a shot at 'im myself.

"To Governor Hoppe," smiled Leon.

Jubal shook his head and said, "To Governor Hoppe."

F.M. came in just as they were drinking down the toast they'd just made.

"I sure am glad you're here, F.M.," said Jubal.

"Oh, you wanted to give me a shot of your rye?" she quipped.

"Not hardly," Stone answered, "but seeing that I'm going to need your services for the next few weeks, why not?"

Jubal reached into the bottom drawer and pulled out another glass, a shot glass that was much smaller than the glasses he and the judge were drinking from. Pouring it half-full he said, "A toast to F.M. Miller and to the excellent training she will offer the Blys."

Stone pushed the shot glass toward Miller. She picked it up and her eyes darted back and forth from Jubal to Leon. "Why do I get the feeling that if I drink this I'm signing up fer something that I didn't sign up fer?"

"Because you are, F.M." smiled Jubal as he poured him and the judge another.

She picked up the glass and threw back her head. Holding the empty glass toward Jubal, she said, "Well, hit me again as long as you're pouring."

Jubal stood to his feet and said, "Reckon I best get home. Nancy will be worried."

Brewster nodded and said, "Same here. Lucy will have a search party out looking for me."

As the men walked toward the door, F.M. cleared her throat loudly, which stopped them both. They turned and looked over their shoulders.

"So, you're not going to tell me what I signed up for?"

Jubal smiled. "Not tonight, but soon."

"Does this have something to do with the Blys by chance?"

Brewster tipped his hat and said, "Goodnight, my lovely niece."

Miller shook her head and said, "Maybe I'll drink the rest of your rye, Jubal. How would you like that?"

"I'll jail you just as sure as you're born, F.M. Make sure to keep a lid on the town tonight, hear?" Jubal said as he and Leon left the room smiling.

Later that night, F.M. made her rounds. When she reached the livery, she saw a man ride up to the hitch on a mule, wrap a bandana around his face, and swing down. As she got closer, she heard an argument going on inside the barn.

"Give me your money, mister, or I'll cripple you for sure." The small fellow holding the pistol pointed it at the liveryman's leg.

"You ain't getting my money, you thief. I work too hard fer it," argued Hank.

"I'm warning you, mister," the man said as he drew back the hammer.

F.M. stepped in the doorway and snatched iron.

"And I'm warning you. Drop it or I'll gun ya."

The man's eyes widened, and he pointed a finger toward F.M. as he continued to hold the gun on Hank. "I'll kill him if you don't pitch that gun in the hay, lady."

"It's Deputy Marshal F.M., and I won't tell you again."

The want-to-be robber hesitated. Miller's Colt belched fire and lead, striking the man in the side. He folded like a cheap tent. Falling to the ground, he cried out in pain as his legs flailed about wildly.

"Hank, do you know this idiot?" she said as reached down and pulled off his bandana.

Grabbing the lantern off the nail, the old liveryman stepped closer and leaned down. As the light hit the young man's face, both F.M. and Hank gasped.

"Why, that's Jake Williams' boy, River. What in tarnation are you doing trying to rob me, son? I ought to take a horse whip to your hide."

"River, I could have killed you," barked F.M. as she pulled back his shirt looking at his wound.

"I wish you would have, Deputy Miller," he replied as he stared up to her with a funeral face.

"What? Why would you say something like that?"

"I can't take it anymore. Ma's sick and Pa says we don't have the money for a doctor."

"You mean you were robbing me so you could pay Doc Reeves to come see your ma?"

River nodded, "Yes, sir." River grimaced in pain as he looked down at his side. "Reckon I'm going to jail. At least there I'm safe from what Pa will do to me when he finds out about this."

"He ain't going to find out," said F.M. sternly as she looked up at the old man. "Ain't that right, Hank?"

"Reckon so," he answered angrily as he reached down to help River up and walked him over to a bale of hay where he and F.M. gently eased him down. The boy was writhing in pain. Of course, F.M. had been gracious in placing her shot. Something told her the man holding the gun a few minutes ago wasn't a hardcore robber. The skinny mule he was riding told her that much. She was right.

"I'll fetch Doc Reeves."

"Like I said, Deputy, I ain't got no money to pay him," rebutted River.

"Ah, who's asking for money, River? Dang fool," she mumbled as she left the barn.

Standing off in the shadows was Eutychus Bly. He could not sleep so he got up and left the hotel. Out walking the town, he saw F.M. making her rounds. A few minutes later, he heard gunfire.

Now standing behind the barn door, he leaned up against the wall pondering what he had just heard. If he had it straight, F.M. had stopped a young man about to do something he would regret the rest of his life. Now she was fetching a doctor for him instead of hauling him off to jail.

Why would she do that given that boy tried to rob the liveryman? Unintentionally, Eutychus Bly was learning one of the first lessons about being a lawman: compassion for fools. He was about to learn his second.

Reeves arrived with bag in hand. F.M. stepped to the doorway and leaned against the frame. She had no intention of letting anybody come in who might go and blab what they had seen. River Williams, grieved over his mother's illness and the fact that he and his family did not have enough money for her to have medical attention, had done a foolish thing. Miller didn't intend on ruining his life over it.

The doc reached into his bag for a pair of scissors. Cutting a swath of material off River's shirt so he could see the wound, F.M. turned away to give the boy some privacy. That's when she noticed a pair of boots poking out from under the barn door that was pulled back.

The next thing Eutychus Bly heard was the click of her Colt's hammer. Then, "Step out of there, mister, and show your face." Miller thought it might be Horace Snider, Waco's town drunk. He often came to the livery to sleep off a drunk in one of the stalls, but she was taking no chances.

"Don't shoot," came a voice in the darkness as a tall man

stepped into the light. To Miller's chagrin, it was Eutychus Bly. She had met him and his family in the diner earlier.

"Mr. Bly," she said with angst in her voice, "what in Sam Hill are you doing here?"

Hank heard the commotion and stepped to the doorway.

"What now, Deputy Miller?" he asked incredulously. Hank was still miffed at River Williams pulling a gun on him and attempting a robbery. He was ready to go to bed but with his barn already turned into an operating room and now a stranger being questioned by the deputy at his door, he wondered if he'd ever get any sleep.

Reeves cleaned the wound thoroughly then wrapped a bandage around River's waist. Then he looked at F.M. then back to the boy. "You know she could have killed you?" Obviously, F.M. had explained what had happened to Reeves on the way to the barn.

"Yes, sir, I know."

"Now, what's this about your ma being sick?" he said as he folded his spectacles and stuffed them in his front pocket.

"She's been ailing something awful. Coughs all the time and can't hardly catch her breath."

Reeves looked down to the ground and shook his head. "Why in thunder am I just now hearing about this?"

"We ain't got no money, Doc. Pa forbid me to fetch you. I figured if I could get some money to pay you, then you'd come."

"Would have come anyway, River. Just sorry your pa is so mule-headed."

"Yes, sir. He is at that."

Reeves raised a finger to River's face. "I want you to get astraddle that mule and get along on home. I'll be there to see your ma around eight o'clock in the morning."

River looked toward the door of the barn nervously for Deputy Miller. She waved Eutychus inside and stared over to Williams.

"How is he, Doc?"

"Just a flesh wound. He's wondering if you're going to lock him up or take my advice and get him aboard his mule and headed home. I'm going out there in the morning to see Sabra."

F.M. nodded and played the part of a hardnosed frontier peace officer.

"I don't know if I have the authority to release him, Doc. He tried to rob Hank at gunpoint. Hank might want to press charges."

Hank stepped forward and started to speak when Reeves stopped him in his tracks by just clearing his throat and tossing him a vicious stare.

Shaking his head, Hank sighed. "Nah, I don't reckon I do." Pointing at River, he said, "But, boy, don't you never try nothing like that again. Now," he said in a softer tone, "do you have any grain to feed that mule of yourn?"

River shook his head and frowned.

"Well, yonder's a half bag of oats. Take it with you and give that mule a good feed when you get home. If your pa says anything about it, you tell him he'll have to deal with me." Hank thumbed his chest.

Doc Reeves and Miller smiled. Then Reeves looked up and asked, "Who are you, mister?"

"I'm Eutychus Bly, Doc. Glad to know you."

Reeves stared at Miller for a moment then reached down and picked up his bag. "Well, Mr. Bly, could you help Hank get River on his mule? I need to speak with the deputy."

"Yes, sir. I'd be proud to."

Reeves motioned for Miller to step outside with him. Then he turned back to her and said, "Did you see that boy's ribcage? Why, he's skin and bones. The Williams need some food or all of them are going to come up sick."

F.M. pulled out a wad of bills and peeled off five of them. "This ought to help, and I'll have more to give come payday."

Reeves took the money in hand. Eutychus saw the exchange as he helped hoist River onto the back of the mule and wondered if F.M. had paid the physician to treat River's wound.

"I'll be out to see your ma in the morning, son. You take it easy going home. I'll change that bandage tomorrow."

River waved and said, "Obliged, Doc, Deputy Miller," as he held the half bag of oats atop the mule's withers.

Reeves walked toward home while Miller said goodnight to Hank. Then she motioned for Eutychus to come with her. As they walked down the streets of Waco, she told him how close he had come to getting shot himself. Eutychus had learned his second lesson about being a peace officer: you need to have a sixth sense about you. Miller somehow sensed that someone else besides her, Hank, River, and the doc were present. Eutychus would have to hone that skill himself, which he fully intended to do.

F.M. rubbed her chin as she looked at Eutychus.

"I'm just a-wonderin' why you folks are in Waco. I know you've moved here from Kansas to give Texas a try. What I don't know is why you've come. Something tells me it's more than just to farm."

Eutychus wasn't sure how much he was allowed to divulge to the deputy, but he could tell right off that she was too smart to beat around the stump. He took a deep breath and spilled his guts. When he was finished, F.M. nodded and said, "Now I know what Jubal and the judge were up to this afternoon."

"Pardon me?" said Eutychus.

"Oh, nothing. I'm just talking out loud. Say, Mr. Bly, you best get some rest. I figure the next few days and weeks are going to be chalked plumb full of new experiences for all of us."

"Obliged, ma'am," Eutychus said as he tipped his hat. "I'm sure I'll see you and the marshal tomorrow. Good night, ma'am."

"Just call me F.M., Mr. Bly. I'm too young for ma'am."

"I sure will, F.M., and I'd be obliged if you'd call me Eutychus."

5

The next morning, Doc Reeves was up early purchasing supplies at the mercantile. It was 7:20 and he was already enroute to the Williams' homestead. He had asked Deputy Miller to ride along with him. Curly Snipes would keep an eye on things until she returned.

When Reeves and Miller arrived, Jake Williams greeted them with a snarl. As they started to climb down from the buggy, he held up his hand and protested their visit. "I ain't got no money, and I'd thank you to get right back in that buggy and head back the way you came."

Reeves, a typical frontier doctor who'd dealt with many cantankerous fellows like Williams, cocked his head sideways and said, "Am I going to have to ask Deputy Miller to shoot you in the leg so that I can examine Sabra?"

"You wouldn't do that, Doc," scowled Williams as he crossed his arms over his chest in a defensive posture.

Miller pulled her pistol and fired a round right between his boots. He jumped a couple of feet off the ground and said, "All right, all right. You can see Sabra." He hollered over his shoulder, "Jake, tell your ma Doc Reeves is here to see her. And rattle your hocks or this loco deputy is liable to cripple me."

Reeves climbed down from the buggy and lifted his bag from under the seat. As he stepped around Jake, he winked at the farmer. Jake reciprocated with a slight grin. Then he stared back at Miller and said, "You blame near shot me in the foot, *Deputy*."

"Yes, sir. And had I been aiming there, I would have."

Jake knew what many in Waco and the surrounding area knew: F.M. Miller was deadly accurate with her six-shooter. She did, in fact, hit what she was aiming at.

Miller looked to the back of the buggy and said, "Mr. Williams, Mr. Riker over-ordered again. Got some supplies back here that are going to go to waste if we don't give them to somebody."

"Now, Deputy Miller, you know I don't accept—"

"Yeah, I know. Charity. Well, this ain't charity. It's love for your neighbor." She threw her hands to her hips. "And Mr. Williams, there's people around these parts that care about you, Miss Sabra, and River. Now, are you going to help me fetch these supplies or make me tote them in myself?"

"River, get out here, boy, and give a hand," Jake barked.

F.M. knew the boy wouldn't be able to lift much with that gunshot wound, the one she had given him just a few hours previously, so she grabbed the sack of flour and hurried into the house. Jake was behind her with a two-pound bag of coffee and a three-pound bag of pinto beans.

"Grab the bread, Jake," she whispered." I'll get the milk, sugar, and potatoes."

River's face lit up with a three-by-nine grin. He was so happy the doctor was tending his mother and to boot, there was now some food in the house for him and his family.

Doc Reeves spent about twenty minutes examining Sabra. When he walked out on the porch, Jake knew it was serious, as did River and F.M.

"What's ailing my Sabra, Doc?" asked Jake.

Reeves eyes blinked several times as he searched for the words to say to the Williams men.

"Jake, Sabra has a serious case of pneumonia. Her lungs are full of fluid. Now, I've given her some medicine. She needs to be kept warm and drink a lot of water, along with broth. I'll be back out here in the morning with some more medicine. Had I come one day later, it would have been too late."

"Well, thank God you came."

"Yes, thank God, and River." Reeves stared over at the boy.

"Yes, sir. He came into town last night to tell me about his ma."

"You did that, son?" Jake asked with surprise.

"Yes, Pa. I hope you're not angry with me. I reckon I disobeyed you and am willing to take my punishment."

"Punishment?" Jake held out his arms to River. "You saved your ma's life." He squeezed his son hard, showing affection he rarely had.

River grimaced in pain but relished his pa's hug anyway.

"Jake, how about you and me going in and seeing Miss Sabra? Would that be all right, Doc?" F.M. asked. She was actually buying the doc time to tend River's wound.

Jake smiled and jumped to his feet. "Come this way, Deputy. My Sabra will be happy to see another female. Reckon she's tired of staring at my ugly mug."

Tears welled up in River's eyes. As he pulled up his shirt for the doc to change his bandage, he smiled and said, "Doc I would have taken ten of these gunshots for what's happened here today."

Reeves smiled with satisfaction. It was moments like these that made being a frontier doctor worth the sweat and tears he had shed for over forty years.

———

Back in Waco, the town was quickly waking up to a new day. The milkman was making his rounds, Mr. Riker was blowing out the wall lanterns outside, and employees of the two diners on Main Street were drawing back the curtains and opening the doors for business.

The Blys had risen early and were coming out of the hotel lobby. Farming families were known for rising early, well ahead of the sun, and getting to their chores before breakfast. However, the Blys had no chores to do so they strolled up one of side of the boardwalks and then the other, taking in all the sights, sounds, and smells of Waco.

"Look, Eutychus," said Myra as she pointed, "that fellow brings the cow right to folks' door." She was of course refer-ring to the milk bottles and cloth-wrapped cheese the dairyman was setting down next to the doors of businesses and homes.

Fred Snider turned to see the Blys staring at him. He waved them over. Reaching for his pocketknife, he cut three small slivers of cheese sitting atop a small wooden turntable. As he handed the pieces to them, he said, "I'm Fred Snider. I reckon you would be the Blys. Heard you had moved here from Kansas. Welcome to Waco."

"Yes, sir. We are the Blys," Eutychus said as he reached into his pocket for money. "How much for the—"

Snider chuckled and shook his head. "Mr. Bly, you don't owe me nothing." Del had almost taken a bite of the cheese and his face lit up with a smile. "That's my payment right there. That smile on your boy's face."

Snider stepped to his wheelbarrow and picked up the handles. "I best rattle my hocks. Folks will be hunting their milk and cheese."

"We're obliged, Mr. Snider, for your kindness," said Myra.

Fred tipped his head and said, "You're mighty welcome, ma'am, and again, welcome to Waco."

"Let's get some breakfast, Myra, and then we'll go down to the mercantile for supplies. I'll need to rent a buckboard." Eutychus shook a finger. "Then I'll visit the gunsmith."

Eutychus' Winchester had burned up during the last fire. He planned to replace it immediately and later purchase a sidearm. As they began walking toward the diner, Jubal Stone came riding by on his big red roan.

"Howdy, Mr. and Mrs. Bly and Del. Sleep well, did you?" he asked as he pulled Red to a stop.

"We did, Marshal," said Eutychus.

Del's eyes lit up as he stared at the roan. Jubal caught his stare and said, "What do you think about him, Del?"

"Oh, he's a dandy, Marshal."

"Well, step down here and introduce yourself to Red. He likes to be stroked."

Del looked up at Eutychus for permission. With a nod from his pa, he jumped down off the boardwalk and held out his hand.

Red sniffed it, then his long pink tongue rolled out as he licked Del's hand. Del chuckled and wiped his hand on his pants. Then he rubbed Red on the nose. The gelding nibbled at him in return.

"I believe he likes you, Del. Come out to the ranch soon and I'll let you ride him."

"You will?" answered the boy excitedly. "You hear that Pa, Ma? The marshal is going to let me ride his horse."

"Now, I'll barter with you, son. You come out to my ranch and do some chores, and we'll put you in the saddle. Is that a deal?"

Again, Del looked to his pa, searching his face for confirmation. Eutychus nodded and Del smiled. Jubal leaned down out of his saddle and extended his hand. "Deal?"

Del reached up and shook it, "Yes, sir. Deal."

Jubal swung down and tied Red to the hitching post in front of the telegraph office. Pointing toward the door, he said, "I have some marshaling business to do. Got to check on my deputy in Burnett. That's a town west of here that we cleaned up recently. Left him there to serve as constable or sheriff until they could get one."

Eutychus put his arm around Myra and gently pulled her his way. "We're going to have some breakfast then pick up supplies." Eutychus stepped toward Jubal. "Saw a blacksmith's shop yonder way." He pointed. "Thought I'd replace that Winchester that got burned in the fire. May even get me a pistol."

Jubal nodded his approval. As he stepped toward the telegraph office door, he turned on his heels. "How about holding off on buying that pistol? I believe I have a rig that you can have."

Bly's face lit up with a smile. "Thank you, Marshal. I'd be proud to accept your offer."

"See you folks directly. By the way, my wife, Nancy, is going to cook super for us. After we get you folks settled in at the Dawson place today, we'll head over to mine."

Myra stepped toward Jubal. "Bless you, Marshal Stone. We were nigh scared out of our wits about leaving Kansas and coming here. But you and the judge and others have made us feel mighty welcome."

"Yeah," said Del. "Even got us a fine slice of cheese from Mr. Snider. He didn't even charge Pa for it."

Eutychus smiled. "I tried to pay him, but he wouldn't have it."

"Fred's a good man, a generous man. He's been serving as Waco's dairyman for over thirty years. We'll get him lined up to bring you folks some milk, butter, and cheese until you can get your own cow."

Eutychus pointed up the boardwalk. As a proud man, he was finding it difficult to accept such generosity. But he knew if he was ever going to be a range detective, he would have to humble himself and accept what others had that he didn't. Right now, that was a place to live, a free pistol, and the expert training that Jubal Stone and others were about to give him and his family.

Two hours later, Jubal caught up with the Blys. They were checking out of the hotel and putting their baggage in the buckboard. Jubal rode up beside their wagon and stopped.

"You folks ready to head out?" As he spoke those words, he saw Doc Reeves and F.M. coming into town in the doc's buggy.

"Reckon they're coming back from the Williams' place. Doc was going to check on Miss Sabra," said Eutychus. "And the boy," he added. Then he stared down at the ground, wishing he'd said nothing.

"The boy?" asked Jubal. "River? What about him? Is he ailing?"

"Oh, nothing," said Eutychus as he stepped over to untie the horse hitched up to the buckboard.

Reeves pulled his buggy to a stop. F.M. climbed down and poked fun at the doc's driving habits.

"Wasn't sure we'd get back to Waco in one piece." She stared back at Reeves and smiled.

"Watch yourself, young lady," warned the doc. Reeves tipped his hat. "Mr. and Mrs. Bly, son, Marshal Stone."

"You've met the Blys, have you, Doc?" asked Jubal.

Reeves rubbed his chin, trying to figure out how to answer that without giving away what happened at the livery the previous night.

"Yeah, we've met."

Jubal stared over to F.M. then back to Reeves. Clearing his throat, he said, "How's River this morning?"

F.M.'s eyes flashed to Jubal. Then she looked to Reeves and finally to Eutychus. Eutychus dropped his head and kicked the dirt, sorry that he'd let the cat out of the bag. So much for being discrete.

"River?" asked F.M. curiously, wondering how much Jubal knew.

Jubal sighed. He smelled a rat. Something had happened, but from Miller's expression he knew it wasn't too serious, so he let it pass, until later.

Reeves quickly picked up the reins and said, "I best tend to my patients. It's going to be a long day." He clucked to his horse

47

and the buggy moved forward. With a wave of the head and a quick look to Miller, he was gone.

Jubal noticed the doc's parting stare at his deputy. He put his hands atop his saddle horn and gave her a stare himself. Miller knew Jubal was suspicious.

"Well," said F.M., "you folks ready to take up farming at the Dawsons'?"

Eutychus quickly answered, "We were just getting set to head out that way. Would you like to come along, Deputy Miller?"

F.M. looked up at Jubal. He nodded and stared down at the gun belt and pistol hanging over his saddle horn. "Reckon training begins today. Drop by and tell Curly where we'll be, then come on out."

"All right, Jubal. Got Razor over there getting fitted for some new shoes anyway." She looked at the Blys. "See you folks directly," and off she went.

When they got to the Dawsons' place, Jubal saw a barouche and knew immediately who it belonged to: Judge Brewster.

"I see you folks already have company." He motioned ahead.

Eutychus looked at Myra who was stroking her hair with her hand and brushing down her dress to make herself presentable. As they got closer, Jubal saw Brewster doing something he'd never seen him do before. He was sweeping off the porch with a broom.

"Well, I'll be," said Jubal as he and the Blys pulled up in front of the house. "I don't believe I've ever seen you pushing a broom, Judge."

Brewster pulled the stump of the cigar from the corner of his mouth and pointed. "And I'll thank to keep this to yourself, Marshal."

The Blys chuckled. Then the door opened to the house. It was Mrs. Lucy and behind her was Nancy toting Monty.

"Mr. and Mrs. Bly, Del, I'd like to introduce you to Mrs. Lucy Brewster and my wife, Nancy. That's my son, Monty, she's got on her hip."

Eutychus stepped down and put out his arms to help Myra down. She stepped toward the ladies and said, "I'm so glad to meet you."

Lucy smiled and said, "Welcome to Waco, Mrs. Bly, and to your new home for now."

Myra stepped up on the porch as Nancy held open the door. When she walked in, she marveled at how clean and orderly everything looked. And there was the smell of lilac in the air. The outside of the house was nice, but the inside was even nicer. The ladies all went inside. The men followed.

After a few minutes of getting acquainted with the house, Jubal motioned toward the door and said to Eutychus and Del, "Let's go out to the barn. As the judge said yesterday, Ted has everything you need to farm this place."

Eutychus put his hand on Del's shoulder and smiled. "Well, let's go have a look, shall we, son?'

"Yes, sir, Pa," answered Del with a smile.

When Jubal pulled open one of the big double doors to the barn, inside was a well-organized wall of tools. A John Deere steel plow was leaned against the wall and well-oiled black harnesses and collars hung on spikes driven into the large posts that supported the barn.

A team of drafts whinnied from the corral.

Brewster came in right behind them. "You figure you could make a go of it here, Mr. Bly?" asked he asked as he lit up another cigar and thumped the match out the door of the barn.

Del quickly ran to the smoking match and stomped on it. The boy was still traumatized from the fire that burned his house and wheat field.

The judge saw the fear in Del's eyes and said, "Thank you, son. I need to be a little more careful with where I throw my match."

Jubal looked away and smiled. He couldn't remember many times when Judge Brewster apologized for anything. In fact, at the moment he couldn't remember one single time.

The men heard a rider. It was F.M. Miller and she and Razor were running at full chisel.

"Now what you do think has that gal in such an all-fired hurry?" asked Leon as he took a drag of his cigar and blew the smoke upward.

Jubal sighed. "You know F.M. doesn't have to have an excuse to ride fast. She's got one speed, and that yonder is it."

Del was mesmerized by F.M.'s ability to ride a horse. He'd never seen a woman ride like that. He hoped that one day he too could sit a fast-moving horse the way she was doing. Del had ridden mules from the barn and to the field and back, but he and his family never had saddle horses, so he didn't know much about equestrianism.

As F.M. pulled up at the barn, Razor reared. Del's eyes widened even more.

Miller swung down and said, "Curly's watching things."

"Ma'am, you sure know how to ride a hoss," said Del.

F.M. dropped the reins and stepped forward. Patting Del on the shoulder, she quipped, "Well, thank you, Del." Then her eye flashed to Jubal. "At least somebody appreciates my abilities."

Jubal pulled off his hat and scratched his head. "Yeah, well, Eutychus and Del, let's get you folks unpacked."

"The marshal's just jealous 'cause I can outride him," fibbed F.M. to Del.

"I heard that, Deputy," snarled Jubal. "Stop stretching the blanket to Del."

Del looked around and smiled at Jubal. Jubal winked at him and warned, "Son, you watch that female yonder. She'll have you believing she's the marshal of Waco instead of me."

"Now, Jubal," she said with a quick glance over her shoulder, "you know you couldn't handle Waco without me." F.M.'s words were truer than they sounded. Miller was Jubal's right hand. If it weren't for her, the marshal would be buried in paperwork and could not do what he did. But Jubal wasn't about to admit it.

"So you tell me," chuckled Jubal.

F.M. tossed Jubal a look of rebuke then she elbowed Del and whispered something to him.

Eutychus looked back at the marshal then to Judge Brewster. Leon shrugged his shoulders and stared ahead. "Don't let either of them fool you, Del. I'm the bull goose of Waco. Don't let nobody tell you otherwise."

"More like the orneriest of Waco," quipped F.M.

"What was that, Deputy?" Brewster asked with squinted eyes. "And just when I was contemplating giving you a raise."

"A raise, Uncle Leon? I've about forgotten what that is."

"Uncle Leon?" said Eutychus.

"Yeah. She's one of mine," smiled Leon.

F.M. turned and smiled at the judge. "I knew you loved me."

Brewster puffed a couple of times on his stogie and said, "Somebody has to."

They all chuckled as they walked to the house.

After getting the Blys unpacked, Jubal pointed to the chairs on the porch. "Take a seat, Eutychus." F.M. leaned against the rails and Brewster sat down in the swing nearby. "Eutychus, it's time we got started. For the next few months, we're going to go whole hog to teach you how to be the best lawman you can be. F.M. is going to teach you how to use a pistol. She's taught a lot of folks over the years. She's the best, but don't say that in front of her. It's liable to go to her head."

F.M. smiled. "Nah, I've got enough in my life to keep me humble."

"When she gets finished showing you how to handle sidearms, we'll move to our next step. But there's something I want you to understand. This business of being a peace officer can turn deadly on the dime."

"Like it did yesterday?" said Eutychus.

"Yes, sir. Like it did yesterday. You've got to listen to us, Eutychus." Jubal pointed to him. "When I give you an order, you obey it without question or hesitation. If I tell you to stay put, you stay put, and don't move. The judge said yesterday you were tempted to do otherwise."

"I just wanted to help you."

"I understand." Jubal waved his hand. "I appreciate your courage, but don't ever disobey one of my commands."

Eutychus dropped his head, sorry that he'd not followed the judge's instructions. He just didn't understand how Marshal Stone could handle two gunmen at one time, although he had done it several times since being chief officer in Waco.

F.M. saw Eutychus' countenance fall and interjected, "Mr. Bly, Jubal Stone has been a law officer since he was sixteen years old. He's got a knack for handling highbinders. I've often wanted to step up beside him and face down the jackals who called him out. But I've learned as you will learn he is more than able to handle himself."

"Obliged, F.M. I bet that hurt to say." Stone grinned.

"More than you'll ever know, Jubal. More than you'll ever know."

Jubal shook his head as he looked to the judge.

"But how will I know when to act and when not to act? I watched Deputy Miller yesterday. She seemed to know exactly what to say and where she needed to be."

"Divide and conquer, Mr. Bly. Divide and conquer," Miller answered.

Eutychus stared curiously, trying to understand what she was saying. Jubal picked up on his confusion.

"I was facing two gun slicks, both planning to draw on me as one. F.M. stepped in and goaded the lead man into facing off with me by himself. Divide and conquer when you can. Gunslingers are all different in one way and all the same in another. They've got a proud streak in them a mile wide. All it takes sometimes is just a little coaxing. Give them a little rope and they'll hang themselves every time."

Eutychus looked a bit overwhelmed. The judge offered his words of encouragement. "Mr. Bly, when Marshal Stone and Deputy Marshal F.M. Miller get finished with you, all of this and more will make sense. How about we just take this a day at a time?"

They all agreed. F.M. pushed off the rails and said, "I'm going out to the barn to find what we can use for a target."

Jubal stepped over to Red and pulled down the gun belt still hanging on the horn. Turning to Eutychus, he said, "Try this on, Mr. Bly."

Eutychus buckled on the belt and looked down at the Colt.

Then he peered over to Jubal as if seeking permission to take hold of it.

Jubal had already emptied the gun from when he took it off one of the men killed in a bank robbery attempt. He pointed down at the pistol and said, "Go ahead and take hold of it, Mr. Bly. It's not loaded."

Eutychus pulled the gun from the holster and dropped it in the dirt. He wasn't expecting it to be so heavy.

Jubal glanced over to the judge and closed his eyes.

Eutychus quickly bent over and picked it up. Embarrassed, he said, "Didn't know it would have that kind of weight." He quickly wiped it down and then stared down the barrel to make sure it was clear of dirt.

Jubal realized in that moment that teaching Eutychus about the proper use of sidearms was going to take some time. He didn't learn what he knew overnight either. He also felt confident that F.M. Miller would be up to the task. She excelled at this. Besides, Jubal's quick draw was unique. When he pulled the trigger on his .44, he did so from the top of his holster. His barrel barely cleared leather. That explained why he was so lightning fast. Most men adept with guns drew their weapons and held them away from their bodies. Not Jubal. Therefore, he would not be the best teacher for Bly.

Eutychus put the pistol back into the holster and said, "Marshal, I don't know much about pistols, but I know a little about how to shoot a Winchester. Shot me a mess of black-tailed jackrabbits, pocket gophers, timber rattlers and a few varmints that were pining for our chickens. But I ain't never used it on a man."

"That'll be my job to teach you, Mr. Bly, if you have the stomach for it."

"Myra and Del, I want them to learn also."

Jubal peered over to Judge Brewster, uncomfortable with the idea of teaching a woman and a boy how to use a rifle as a lethal weapon.

"Tell me, Eutychus," said Jubal. "When you decided to take on becoming a range detective for the state of Kansas, did you have in mind including your wife and son in the job?"

"Excuse me, Marshal," said Myra as she pushed open the screen door. "I can answer that." She joined the men on the porch. Normally Myra would not have been so assertive, but Stone's question prompted it.

Jubal and the judge stared over to Myra. Eutychus did as well.

"I told you some of what happened in the past with the Blys. I've thought many times since then that had the womenfolk and older children known how to handle guns, perhaps more settlers would be alive today."

"Could be, ma'am," said Jubal, "or a mite more of them could be dead. The fact that those killers went after the men tells me they didn't see the women and children as a threat."

"That's right. But I will never again stand idle and watch what we worked so hard for go up in smoke without a fight. My husband attempted to confront the man behind destroying our place. Asked him to pay for the damages. It almost got him killed. Never again."

Del stepped around his mother. Clearing his throat, he looked up at Stone and with teary eyes said, "Marshal, I saw what losing our farm did to my pa, and I couldn't do a blessed thing about it. I figure with a little know-how about the use of this"—he raised the new Winchester Eutychus had purchased that morning in the air—"we won't be such easy pickings next time."

Jubal nodded and smiled. He liked the moxie of Myra and Del and remembered recently how Nancy had been forced to use the family's shotgun through the window of their home to keep a killer at bay.

"Well, Del, tell me, did your pa buy any ammunition for that smoke stick?"

Del stepped back into the house and picked up a box of cartridges. "Yes, sir, he did."

"Bring your rifle and your cartridges with you when you come to the ranch this evening for supper. No time like the present to start learning."

"Yes, sir," said Del as he leaned the rifle against the wall and stepped forward to shake Jubal's hand. Then Del disappeared inside to unpack his belongings.

"That's a fine boy you've got there, Mr. Bly," said Jubal.

"Obliged, Marshal. As you can see, my family and I are ready to learn. When we return to Kansas, we don't want go back the same people."

6

F.M. located some old feedbags in the barn and some paint. She called Eutychus out to the barn to nail a couple of boards together to be used as a backdrop for target practice. As he walked her way, he pulled the gun out of the holster and loaded the chambers with cartridges. Then he stepped inside to find F.M. dabbing white paint on a burlap bag.

"Let's set us up a target out behind the barn," Miller said as she glimpsed him coming in. When they got to where F.M. thought was a good spot, she told Eutychus to drive the wood in the ground. Then she tacked the burlap bag to the cross-shaped wood and stepped back about twenty feet.

"Come on over here, Mr. Bly," said F.M. as she pointed down at the ground next to her. When he got there, F.M. snatched iron and nailed the target just a half-inch from the white paint spot that served as the bullseye.

"Dang, that's some good shooting, Deputy Miller," said Eutychus as he stared hard at the target with glee. "Reckon I'll ever be as good as you with this here pistol?" He pointed down at the Colt in his holster.

"As good as me?" F.M. asked.

"Yeah," said Eutychus.

"No, but when I get finished with you, Mr. Bly, you'll be able to hit what you aim at and do it fast."

"Ma'am." Eutychus shook his head and snapped his finger. "I mean Deputy Miller."

"Just call me F.M." She rolled her eyes.

"F.M., do you like smoked ham?"

"Smoked ham? I reckon so, as much as the next person, I guess. Why do you ask?" she said with wrinkled face.

"You teach me to shoot like you, and ol' Eutychus is going to smoke you the best ham you ever wrapped your mouth around. Nobody smokes a ham like me."

F.M. knew Eutychus was a proud man and that he wanted her to know he planned to pay her back for her time. Miller nodded. Then she motioned to his pistol and said, "Well, let's get at it. Now, yank that shooter and aim it toward the target."

Eutychus crouched as he had seen F.M. do and grabbed for the pistol. His long fingers went past the holster. He missed the pistol handle altogether. He wrestled with the holster with both hands until he found the gun and got it shucked.

F.M. waved a hand. "Hold up, Eutychus. Let's start over. Now, slowly lower your hand to your gun and run your fingers over the butt of it. That's where that gun is always going to be. When you drop your hand, it needs to be less than two inches from the grip. You've always got to know where your gun is. Now, let's try it again."

Eutychus looked down to the Colt. Miller quickly reprimanded him. "Don't look down, Eutychus. Never look down.

You're wasting time when you do that and letting your opponent know that you're unsure of yourself."

Bly nodded then started to look down but corrected himself. Then he lowered his hand slowly and touched the grip.

"That's good. Now I want you to close your eyes and try that again."

Eutychus did as she told him and eased his hand down his side until he bumped against the grip.

"Good. Now, we're not going to worry much more today about you drawing your pistol. But I do want you to practice finding your gun with your hand for the next few days. Wear that iron everywhere you go from now on, except inside your house. And practice finding it with your hand."

F.M. crouched and her gun seemed to leap out of the holster. Eutychus shook his head. "You're near as fast as the marshal, F.M."

"No, sir. Ain't nobody as fast as Jubal Stone with a Colt. There's a lot of dead men on Boot Hill and across Texas who thought otherwise."

"You think you'll ever be as fast as the marshal, F.M.?"

"No. Jubal has what's called a natural fast draw. He shoots right out of the holster. There's only a few men alive can hit what they aim at drawing that way."

Eutychus lowered his hand to his gun and his fingers wrapped around the handle smoothly.

"That's good, Eutychus. You just keep at it. It will become as natural as reaching for a doorknob or buttoning your shirt or pulling on your hat." She chuckled. "Or smoking a ham. Now, let's see how you hold your gun when you pull the trigger. Take your pistol from the holster, cock back the hammer, and pull the trigger as you aim at the target."

Eutychus did as F.M. told him but when he pulled the trigger, the gun went off and jumped out of his hand.

"When did you load that shooter?" she asked angrily. "I thought Jubal said it was empty."

"Yes, ma'am, it was, but I put the bullets in it on the way out to the barn."

F.M. shook her head and bent down and retrieved the gun. Blowing the dirt off it, she emptied the gun of the cartridges. "Lesson number one: always treat a pistol as if it's loaded." Miller looked back toward the house to make sure no one was looking.

"All right, Eutychus, here's the next lesson. Whenever you take hold of a pistol, you hold it tight, so tight that if somebody tried to take it out of your hand, they couldn't. Let's try that."

She handed him back the gun then grabbed the barrel. He held on tight until she stopped.

"That's it." Then she held out her hand. "Now let me have you gun."

Eutychus quickly shoved it into her hand. Miller shook her head. "Lesson number three: Don't never let another man or woman take your gun, unless you're being arrested by the law. You understand?" she asked as she handed him back the Colt.

"Yes, ma'am, I do."

"Now, let me put some bullets in your gun and see how well you can hit the target."

Eutychus again surrendered his gun to her without hesitation. She stared at him until he jerked it back out of her hand.

"Dang it, F.M., you're wilier than a fox."

"Yeah, Eutychus, and some folks are dumber than a fence post." She smiled and so did he.

"Now, load your gun, and I want to see if you can hit the target. You need some help?" she asked as she reached for the Colt. This time, however, Eutychus was on to her.

"No, ma'am, I don't," he said as he turned his body in front of her to block her advancement. "But thanks for offering."

"Finally," F.M. whispered under her breath. She pointed at the target. "Thumb back the hammer and take aim, just like you'd do with your rifle. When you have that white spot in your sights, squeeze that trigger, but make sure you've got a tight grip on that shooter. I don't want to get lead poisonin'."

Eutychus chuckled then he crouched a bit and held the gun in the air. Drawing back the hammer with his thumb, he took aim. Taking a deep breath, he squeezed the trigger until the barrel blazed. The loud explosion hurt his ears.

"Well, you did hit the burlap, but you're a fer piece from the white spot. Let's try again. This time, when you take a breath, let it out then squeeze the trigger."

Eutychus raised the gun again, thumbed back the hammer, found the white spot in his sights, and took a deep breath. Letting it out, he squeezed the trigger as he held the gun firmly in his hand. This time, he struck the target about eight inches from the white spot.

"You're getting closer, Eutychus. This time, I want you to bend your knees a little and lean forward just a tad. Let's try it again."

Eutychus did as Miller said. He bent his knees slightly and leaned forward. Drawing back the hammer, he repeated what he'd done before. When the pistol fired, Eutychus lowered it and stared at the target. He was about five inches to the right of the bullseye. He turned to F.M. for her response.

She smiled. "About three more shots and you'll be in the money, Mr. Bly."

She stepped toward him. "Now, remember, the more you shoot the gun, the hotter the barrel will get and less accurate you're shooting will be. Let me check that barrel for heat." She held out her hand.

Eutychus shook his head. "Nobody takes my gun, ma'am." He felt the barrel. "It's warm but not hot. I reckon it's fine."

"You're on your way, Mr. Bly. Now, you need to practice your shooting every day. I'll be back out here tomorrow afternoon. Remember, we're just working on accuracy right now, not speed. Speed's important, but if it's not matched with accuracy, you're spittin' in the wind."

Jubal stepped out on the porch and gave a whistle. Miller answered back with her own.

"Let's go, Eutychus. That concludes your first sidearm lesson."

As they walked toward the house, Myra and Del climbed down the steps. Del said, "How did you do, Pa?"

"Well, son, I figure about five empty boxes of shells and I'll be hitting what I'm aiming out. What do you think, Deputy Miller?"

Miller nodded. "Five boxes. That's sounds about right to me."

"Come in and look at the house, Eutychus," said Myra as she grabbed him by the arm. "They done fixed it up so nice for us and just take the smell of that lilac." She breathed in deeply and closed her eyes. Eutychus smiled at Myra's expression. He had not seen his wife smile in a while.

Judge Brewster, Mrs. Lucy, and Nancy were coming out of the house as they were going in. The three of them turned to watch the reaction of Eutychus. Earlier he had come inside but didn't really have time to look around because Jubal had suggested they go out to the barn.

"My, oh my," he said as he walked from room to room with Myra. Del was beside himself because the room he'd be staying in had a nice big bed flanked by a window on each side. A lantern sat on the small table next to the bed. Del loved to read and was excited about having his own lantern.

Judge Brewster climbed down the steps and helped Lucy up into the barouche. Then he untied the horse and got up in the seat beside Lucy. Raising his hat, he said, "Well, seeing that we weren't invited to supper at the Stones', I reckon we'll amble back to town."

"Now, Judge," Nancy scolded. "You're stretching the truth a mite."

"Yes, he is," said Lucy as she elbowed him in the side. "The judge has a deposition he's got to finish this evening. We're sorry we won't be able to make it."

As they rode out, Jubal and his family would not be far behind.

Myra was now holding Monty as Del made faces at him. Nancy smiled as she watched the two boys interact.

"We best head for home, Jubal," said Nancy, "if I'm going to get supper on the table."

"Sure hate for you folks to go to all that trouble," said Eutychus.

"Oh, nonsense." Nancy waved a hand. "We are so happy to have you and your family join us."

F.M. cleared her throat. "Well, since I wasn't invited to the Stones' for supper, me and Razor are going to scat for town."

"F.M., you know..."

"I'm just fibbing you, Nancy. I best get into town and see if it's still standing. If I know Curly, he's liable to be doing his blacksmithing in the marshal's office. Probably has black soot all over Jubal's desk by now."

"He best not be," snarled Jubal, "but I wouldn't put it past him. You sure that's not the only reason you want to go check up on him, Deputy Miller?"

F.M. turned three shades of red. Jubal knew just how to get her goat, and from the expression on her face, that's exactly what he'd just done.

"Jubal." Nancy tossed him a look of rebuke.

He smiled and said, "I keep telling her if she'd get hitched to Mr. Snipes, she'd never have to pay for horseshoes again."

"And I keep telling you, Jubal Stone... Oh, forget it," Miller said, exasperated. Then she turned to Eutychus and pointed. "You practice finding that gun with your hand and shooting. I'll be back here tomorrow afternoon around four o'clock." She looked back at Jubal. "That is if I haven't married up with Curly Snipes by then."

Nancy again looked to Jubal sternly. She knew F.M. was on the edge of boiling over. That tickled Jubal even more. He wiped his face of his smile and headed for the door. Miller came out behind him with a scowl.

Jubal turned to her and his expression changed to serious. "You heard anything from Tanner lately? Wonder how he's faring in Burnett?"

Now a chance to get back at Jubal, she said, "Yeah, I did. I believe he's found a home there. I look for him to become their permanent lawman."

"Sure enough?" said Jubal with a concerned look. "Don't know that I would have left him there if I'd known that."

"I'm just fibbing you, Jubal. But I did hear from Tanner. Got a wire just before I came out here. Everything's peaceful in Burnett. He's probably getting better pay there than Waco deputies do."

"Now, F.M." Jubal waved a finger. Then Nancy came out with Monty on her hip. She looked at Jubal then to FM.

"Am I interrupted something?"

"No, ma'am," answered Miller. "Jubal was just telling me how he plans to ask the judge to give me a raise."

Nancy smiled and looked down to the porch. "Oh, well, Jubal, we better go." She smiled.

Jubal frowned at F.M. then shook his head. Climbing down the steps, he helped Nancy aboard. Then he unhitched the buggy horse and crawled up beside Nancy. Now he was the one who looked to be on the prod. He tipped his hat to the Blys and tapped the reins to the horse's rump and they were off.

Miller smiled as she looked toward Jubal.

"Two can play at that game, Marshal."

Myra, Del, and Eutychus stood there staring, amused at the camaraderie between the deputy and the marshal.

Miller climbed aboard Razor and said, "It's good to have you here, Mr. and Mrs. Bly, Del." She touched her hat then spurred Razor forward. He left out of there like a bullet from a gun.

Del hurried down the steps as if he was going to follow F.M. He just wanted to get one last glimpse of the fast riding she was doing. He hoped soon he'd be able to sit a horse like the female deputy who was leaving behind a cloud of dust.

"Come on, son," said Myra. "We've got to get cleaned up to go to the Stones."

"Yes, ma'am," he said as he continued to stare in the direction Deputy Miller had ridden. Now she was gone.

Del turned on his heels and said, "Marshal Stone told me I could ride his red roan."

"Well, son, that's just fine," said Eutychus, "but let's don't ask him today, all right?"

Del was disappointed with his pa's words. In the back of his mind, he had planned to talk to Jubal about riding. Now he would have to wait.

Eutychus walked toward the barn, dropping his hand to the gun as he went. Myra called out to her husband. He didn't even respond. She smiled as she watched him practicing with his hand to the gun.

"Mr. Bly!" she yelled.

He stopped in his tracks and turned toward the house. She waved him toward her.

"What's wrong, honey, and why did you call me Mr. Bly?"

"Nothing's wrong, and I called you Mr. Bly because you didn't respond to Eutychus."

"Reckon I was focused too much on what the deputy told me to work on."

Myra smiled. She loved Eutychus and knew he was already doing his best to get trained up in sidearm use. The move from Kansas was a hard one, but Myra, Eutychus, and Del knew exactly why they were in Texas.

"We need to get cleaned up and start toward the Stones."

"Yes, ma'am, Mrs. Bly," smiled Eutychus. Then he stepped up on the porch and kissed his wife.

"Eutychus." She blushed. "Not out here. Del's about the place."

"Well, I ain't ashamed to let people know I love you, Myra Bly."

She smiled warmly and bumped him on the arm. "What am I going to do with you?"

This is the first time either one of them had genuinely smiled in the last few months. Life had been hard on the Blys. In fact, there were a few times, although neither admitted it to one another, that Myra and Eutychus wondered if there was any hope for them to be happy. Now that they were in Texas and far removed from the trauma they had experienced in Kansas, they felt relieved and even hopeful. With the quality of law officers training them, they were certain they'd learn the skills they needed to do the job the governor wanted them to do.

7

That evening, the Blys arrived at the Stones. Eutychus was wearing his pistol and on Myra's lap lay his brand new Winchester he'd purchased in the hardware store. He had visited the gunsmith, but he seemed to be a little on the proud side with his prices. Therefore, Eutychus found a better deal at the dry goods store.

Jasper barked and moved slowly down the steps to greet the guests. "Hush up, Jasper," ordered Jubal and the cur disappeared under the porch of the house.

Del watched with amusement. He'd wanted a dog for a long time, but because times were hard, Eutychus told him that they couldn't afford to feed another mouth.

"Y'all get down and stay a spell," said Jubal as he held Monty like a loaf of bread. Monty didn't seem to mind it. In fact, he was cooing and smiling as the Blys got down out of the buckboard.

Myra smiled as she saw Monty dangling from Jubal's arm. Nancy came out just in time to give her husband a look, that special kind of life-changing glance that only a wife can give her husband. He got the message and changed positions with Monty.

Del came up the steps and tickled Monty's feet. Jubal held him out and said, "You want to hold him, Del? He sure seems to cotton to you."

Del looked back at his ma. She nodded and said, "Just be careful. Make sure you support his head now."

The two of them sat down in one of the porch rockers and got better acquainted. Nancy even remarked how much Monty took to Del.

Out in the corral, Red nickered followed by Powder, then June Bug. Big Dan, Jubal's dun stallion, pawed the floor of the barn, demanding to be fed.

"I was just about to give them jug heads some oats. You fellows want to come along?" Jubal knew that Del was infatuated with horses. The way he'd taken to Red earlier that morning told him all he needed to know.

"Can we, Pa?" Del asked as he stood with Monty in his arms.

"Hold up there, son," said Myra as she extended her hands to take the baby. "I don't believe he's ready to take up with the horses yet."

"Let's go take a gander at the marshal's remuda, Del. Looks to be some prime horse flesh if you ask me."

Jubal had already taken a liking to the Blys. They were a humble family just trying to find their way in life. And the story he had heard about their troubles ingratiated them to him even more. Angry is what he was. He'd like nothing more than to ride out to the Kansas Plains and say howdy to Herman Stokes with his .44 Colt. However, he knew the best thing he could do right now was train Eutychus to be the best lawman that he could be.

Walking out to the barn, Jubal glanced over to Eutychus. "I see you're wearing your gun."

Bly dropped his hand atop the grip. "Yes, sir. I know just where it is."

"That Deputy Miller knows a few things about sidearms."

"She sure does," smiled Bly. "I asked her if she'd ever be as fast as you with her pistol."

Stone smiled. "What'd she say?"

"Said there ain't nobody as fast as Marshal Jubal Stone. Said you have a unique way of drawing and hitting what you aim at. Fast draw right out of your holster. I seen that myself this morning in town with that gunman."

Jubal didn't like attention or flattery, especially when it came to handling his shootin' piece. He had never gotten accustomed to having to kill a man and hoped that he never would.

"Mr. Bly," Jubal said as he stopped walking. "I only use my weapon when it's absolutely necessary. I take no pride in killing men or even being able to outdraw those who have pulled iron on me. Unfortunately, it's the only way I've been able to stay alive."

"Marshal Stone," said Eutychus. "I hope I never have to kill a man, but I want sit idly by and let one kill me or my family. I've tried that way of life, and it's left me with many regrets."

Del turned back toward Jubal and his pa. "Marshal, is it all right if I step over there and pet Red? He sure seemed to like it this morning."

"Why, sure, Del. I'll go you a better one than that. I'll let you on a little secret."

"What's that, Marshal?" the boy asked with bated breath.

"I'll tell you something he likes even more than to be rubbed: eating oats. Come on into the barn with me and we'll fetch some. Then you pour some in the trough out here and you'll have the whole herd coming to you."

Del did as Jubal said and in a couple of minutes, he was carrying a burlap sack that was about a quarter way full. He dumped the oats between the rails and into the trough. The horses did as Jubal said they would. They came to Del and quickly.

Big Dan was pacing back and forth in his stall, protesting having to wait for his supper. Jubal scooped out some oats and pushed them through a small opening in the boards. The stallion pinned his ears and stepped toward the feed. Jubal spoke firmly to him as a rebuke.

"I don't like bad manners in a horse or a man. I won't tolerate it," he said as if speaking of Big Dan, but he was really communicating one of his core values to Eutychus.

"What do you mean by that, Marshal?" asked Bly.

"Sit yonder on that hay bale and let's jaw a minute."

As Eutychus sat down, Jubal began teaching him some of the things he would need to know about handling difficult men.

"Men are men wherever you go, Eutychus. Most of them are all mouth. They talk like they're ten feet tall, like to bully people around. But I've found when you let them know you won't be pushed around, you won't be laid hand upon, and you won't tolerate their bad behavior, most of them give up the fight."

"And those who don't?"

"You have to brace 'em. Or else when you take a step backward, they'll fill up your boot prints."

Del was listening to Jubal's every word as he stood and rubbed Red and Powder on their foreheads as they munched their oats. The marshal's words were as tantalizing to his ears as much as the sound of the horses chewing their oats.

"I'm a quiet man, Marshal. Have been all my life. I don't go around looking for fights, but I know now that a man who won't stand up will get stomped on, along with his family."

"Eutychus," said Jubal. "I'm going to be straight up with you. The frontier, whether it's Kansas or Texas, is a hard land. And those who serve as lawman have to be hard themselves. I don't mean cruel. I mean tough."

"You wonder if I'm tough enough, right, Marshal?"

"That's right, Eutychus. I..."

Del suddenly stopped grooming the horses and looked in the direction his dad and the marshal were talking. He rushed right over to Jubal and said, "Marshal Stone, my pa is tough, and you shouldn't say otherwise."

Eutychus stood up and put a hand to Del's shoulder. "Son, what's got into you?" he asked as he gently shook him.

Tears streamed down Del's face and he breathed hard. Then he pointed toward Jubal. "He shouldn't have said those things about you, Pa."

Jubal stood to his feet and said, "I'll tell you what's gotten into him, Eutychus: pride. Pride for his pa. He knows you can do this, but my question is, do you? Do you, Eutychus Bly? Is this something you are willing to give your whole heart to? If not, don't waste my time or yours."

Del looked up into his pa's face. "Pa?"

Eutychus stepped away from Del and Jubal and stared at the back wall of the barn. Jubal could tell he was wrestling with his inner thoughts. Something was holding him back.

"Pa?" said Del as he stared at the back of Eutychus.

Still Eutychus didn't respond. He just stared at the back wall as if the answer was hanging up somewhere between the sickle, the shovel, and the big logging chain.

Jubal looked down to the floor then he stared across the barn to Eutychus. Sighing deeply, he shook his head. "Mr. Bly, I think you and your family ought to think about settling here in Texas, maybe find your own place and sink down roots. Being a range detective, well... that just may be above your bend. How about we go and have supper?"

Eutychus' whole body began to quiver as he breathed harder and harder. Then he turned on his heels and rushed over to Jubal. Grabbing up two handfuls of shirt, he picked Stone up off the ground and said through gritted teeth, "I didn't come to Texas to set down roots. I came to be trained as a range detective. Now if you ain't going to do it, I'll find someone who will." Then he released Jubal and stepped back.

Jubal brushed down his shirt and stared sternly at the tall, lanky man. Jubal Stone wasn't the kind of man who would allow another man this kind of latitude, but inside he knew Eutychus Bly had just turned a corner.

Smiling, he said as he nodded, "You just may make a Kansas range detective yet, Mr. Bly. Del, fetch that rifle and them box of shells. Your pa's got some shooting to do."

Del yelled, "Yes, sir!" Then he bounded out of the barn. The horses jumped back from the trough a bit skittish but quickly returned for the remaining heads of grain they had overlooked.

Eutychus stepped over to Jubal and held out his hand.

"Thank you, Jubal. And... I'm sorry about the shirt." There was a rip just under the collar where Eutychus had took hold of him.

"I ain't, Eutychus. You're a strong man to lift me off the ground, and it's going to take you being strong in a lot of ways to be who you need to be, especially when you get back to Kansas."

Del had the rifle in one hand and a box of cartridges in the other as he came back into the barn grinning from ear to ear.

"Here they are, Marshal." He handed both to Jubal.

Eutychus stepped up and pulled his son to his chest. "I'm proud of the man you're becoming, Del. You and your ma, well... I can't rightly think how I could make it without you two."

The boy's face lit up like the sky on the fourth of July. He knew his father was a strong man in more ways than one. But when Del saw him lift Marshal Stone off the ground by the shirt, he was in awe, just as any boy ought to be of his father. He was also glad that the marshal didn't take offense to what he had said and what his pa had done.

A few minutes later, a Winchester thundered off in the distance. Eutychus Bly was learning the skill of shooting a rifle long range. His hunting skills came in handy for small game close by but being a range detective on the Kansas Plains would require him to master the use of a rifle at over four hundred yards or more.

Jubal had set up three targets: one at a hundred yards, one at two hundred, and one at three hundred. Eutychus hit the closet one several times, but when he aimed for the two-hundred-yard target, he missed altogether. After firing three more times at it, Jubal suggested that was enough for the day. They headed to the house for dinner.

Over the next several weeks, Deputy Miller continued training Bly to use a handgun. He had even hit the bullseye a couple of times and seemed to know where his gun was when he dropped his hand to it.

"You're doing well, Mr. Bly. Now, we move to speed."

Eutychus nodded, communicating that he was ready.

"I want you to empty your gun and put the cartridges in your pocket. Then slip your pistol back into the holster."

Bly did as F.M said.

"Fish out them six bullets and let me see them," she said.

Eutychus reached into his pocket and opened the palm of his hand. F.M. stepped over and counted all of them. "Six it is. I just didn't want to get shot." Then she snatched her Colt from the holster and removed her bullets. Holding them in the palm of her hand, she counted six.

Bly smiled remembering a couple of weeks previously how Miller about jumped out of her skin when his gun fired at the target. She thought it was empty.

"Step over in front of me. Now, I want you to imagine that I had just shot up the town of Waco and you're the deputy. You can tell I'm a gunman. You step off the boardwalk and into the street. What do you say to me? How would you handle that?"

"I reckon I'd ask the man what he was doing and why?" Eutychus held up his palms as if he was in discussion with the gunman.

F.M. drew her pistol and said sternly, "I just killed me a lawman." Then she stepped forward and scolded Bly who looked like a puppy that had just been caught coming out of the hen house with an egg in his mouth.

"Eutychus, you don't ever move your hand away from your gun when confronting a man that's acting a fool with his gun. When you raised your hand a second ago asking me what I was doing and why, you were a good foot from your pistol."

F.M. and Jubal continued to work with Eutychus, teaching him all they could to prepare him for his job ahead. They had taught him about guns. Now, Eutychus needed to master equitation.

Eutychus had been raised around livestock—pigs, cows, chickens, and mules. However, when it came to horses, he was an amateur. Riding on the backs of the plow mules his father used in the fields was a whole lot different than sitting in leather astraddle a spirited horse. And a spirited horse is exactly what Bly would need to do his job on the Kansas Plains and Prairies.

As Jubal rode into Waco, he had some several things on his mind. He and Deputy Miller has some paperwork to finish for the judge and he needed to get with the freight manager about some army payrolls that would be coming through town. Another thing on his mind though was finding a horse for Eutychus. After all, a frontier lawman was only as good as the pistol in his holster and the horse up under him. Both were vitally important, not only to his job but keeping him alive.

Jubal finished up the paperwork with F.M. She asked if he wanted her to fetch it to Brewster.

"Obliged, but I've got some other business with the judge, so I'll take it to him."

Jubal crossed the street and headed up the boardwalk to Brewster's office. He tapped on the door and heard Mrs. Creel walking across the hardwood floors. Pulling the door open, she smiled and said, "Marshal Stone. Good morning, and please come in."

Mrs. Edna Creel was always the epitome of what a professional secretary ought to be. She represented the judge well with her perfect manners, accentuated by her stylish clothing. Her nails were always glossy and every hair on her head seemed to be in the perfect place.

Stone removed his hat and stepped inside.

Mrs. Creel looked at the papers stashed under Jubal's arm and said, "I take it you'd like to see the judge?"

"Yes, ma'am, if he's not asleep."

"Marshal Stone," she said in a slight corrective tone.

"Or drunk."

"I heard that, Jubal," came a deep voice from down the hall.

"I meant for you to, Judge." Jubal smiled.

Brewster stepped to his door and waved Jubal inside. Mrs. Creel followed and asked, "Would you gents like a cup of coffee?"

Jubal always enjoyed Brewster's coffee: Arbuckle's, the finest on the market.

"Yes, ma'am, I would love a pot or two," smiled Jubal.

The judge frowned. "Bring me a cup full and him one half full, Edna."

Jubal smiled back at Mrs. Creel and shook his head as he set down the small stack of papers on Brewster's desk and sat in the chair across from him. Pointing, he said, "There they are, Judge."

"Fine, fine, Jubal," Leon said as he rubbed his hand across them. "I'm trying to get caught up on some of the cases that are backlogged. How's our Kansas range detective doing?"

"He's come a long way, Judge. Fact is, Eutychus is one of the reasons I came over here this morning."

"Yeah, that and to swill down some of my good coffee."

"Well, yes, sir. Every chance I get." Jubal pointed. "Say, seems I remember a certain judge promising me a bag of this stuff." Stone took a sip of his coffee and waited for Brewster's reply.

"Now, Jubal. You know dang well I brought you that bag a week ago."

"Oh, yeah. So, you did, Judge. My mistake."

"You must think I've got that old-timer's disease where I can't remember anything."

"Well, I was kind of hoping you'd forgot about the coffee."

"Not a chance, Marshal. Not a chance," Leon said with moxie.

Jubal and Leon shared a special bond together. They were always goading one another about something.

"Now about Eutychus, Judge."

"Yeah."

"He needs a horse, a good horse, a horse the cut of Red and Powder."

Brewster chuckled. "Thought you said a good horse."

Jubal raised a finger of rebuke. The judge waved and said, "All right, I won't badmouth your horses even though they come from mule stock."

"Well, now, I see another bag of Arbuckle's in my future."

"Why do you say that?"

"Because it will cost you another bag to keep me from telling Hiram Skinner you said that a colt from his stallion was from mule stock."

Brewster pounded the table with his fist and said, "Dang if I ain't going to go broke paying you off in coffee not to divulge secrets. You know that's blackmail, don't you?"

"Yes, sir, I do. And I'll expect my coffee soon or else."

"All right, back to Eutychus needing a horse."

"Reckon you could wire Governor Hoppe and get him to spring for one of Mr. Skinner's horses for Bly? I figure by the time Eutychus heads back to Kansas, he and the horse will be ready."

Brewster leaned forward over his desk and said, "Marshal, you go out to Hiram's and pick out the best he has. I'll make sure he gets paid. Hoppe owes us."

Jubal smiled. "He'll need tack to go with the animal."

"Go down to Percy's and get what you need. Tell him to put it on my bill."

Stone stood to his feet and said, "I sure could use a new saddle myself. Now that I've got me an open account at Percy's, it's a good time to get one. What would you say to that, Judge?"

Jubal waited for Brewster to throw a fit. He knew it would be worth a laugh.

"I'd swear out a warrant for your arrest and have you serve yourself. Now get out of my office so I can get to these cases. I've already got me a headache brewing."

Grinning, Jubal gulped down what was left in his cup and stood to his feet as he pulled on his hat. As he turned to the door, he said, "Eutychus Bly is going to make a good Kansas lawman. And I tell you another thing, Judge. You ain't never seen a twelve-year-boy shoot a rifle like Del Bly. He took to it like a duck to water."

"Sure enough?" Brewster asked, shaking his head. Then he looked at Jubal. "I just hope he never has to use those skills on a man."

"Me too, Judge. Me too. But, if he has to, he'll know how."

Later that day, Jubal took a ride out to Hiram Skinner's homestead. Hiram raised some of the finest horses in Texas. Powder, Jubal's blue roan, was sired by Skinner's stallion, Chet, and the dam was a fine-blooded brood mare named Matilda.

As Jubal rode up, he saw Hiram standing in the entrance of the barn with a pitchfork in his hands. He wheeled Powder in that direction and stopped at the hitch.

"Well, howdy, Marshal," said Hiram as he leaned the pitchfork against the wall. "Climb on down and visit a spell. That sure is a fine animal you're riding."

"Good day, Hiram. How you keeping?" Jubal asked as he tethered Powder to the rail.

"Can't complain," he said with a smile, then he leaned in and said, "but I do it anyway."

Jubal looked back to Chet in the back stall. "How's that stud of yourn? Is he earning his keep?"

"Ol' Chet's pulling his freight. Got me two new colts, both born last week. How about that dun of yours? You bred him to any of your mares yet?"

"No, sir, not yet, but I figure to put Big Dan to work in the next few days. Got one mare showing some interest."

Jubal looked across Hiram's pasture to his herd of horses, about eleven in all.

"You in the market for a horse, Marshal?"

"Could be. I need one the cut of Powder."

As Jubal continued looking at the herd, he spotted a gelding that looked very familiar. It was a big, long-legged pinto.

"Ain't that Salice's horse, that pinto yonder?"

Hiram smiled and said, "You do know your horses, Marshal Stone. And yes, that is your brother's horse."

"Well, what's it doing in your pasture?"

"He goes where I go," came a voice from behind him. Jubal knew instantly who it was.

Turning on his heels, he exclaimed, "Well, you rascal! Slipped into town and don't tell nobody, even your kin."

"I didn't go into Waco. I heard they had a hard-nosed marshal there that didn't fancy strangers visiting." Salice was joshing, but what he was saying was true. Jubal Stone and his deputies, if they had their preference, would be happy to close the town off to strangers, given the trouble they'd had with many who had passed through Waco.

The brothers shook hands. Then Hiram cleared his throat and said, "I'll be having words with you, Marshal."

Jubal turned and looked at Hiram curiously. He knew by the smirk on his face that Skinner wasn't serious. "What's the problem, Hiram?"

"That one right there." He pointed at Salice. "Done stole the heart of my Maddie. As much as I tried, she still done took up with a Mexican."

Salice did not take offense to Skinner's words because he knew he spoke to them in jest, being that Hiram's wife, Maria, was full-blooded Mexican. "I used to be the only man in Maddie's life. Now I reckon I'm playing second fiddle."

"Now, Pa. You know nobody will ever take your place," came a female voice behind Salice. It was Maddie Skinner. She was dressed to ride, and ride this young lady knew how to do. Maddie walked up to Hiram and took him by the arm. Rising up on her tiptoes, she gave him a peck on the cheek. Then she stepped over and did the same with Salice.

"Good morning, Marshal Stone. How are you?" she asked with a pleasant smile.

"Very well, Maddie. But I see you're still running with this highbinder." He motioned to Salice.

"Now, look here, gents," Maddie said as she put her hands to her hips. "I ain't going to stand by and listen to you run down my man."

Salice put his arm around her and said, "Don't let her size fool you. You know what they say? Dynamite comes in small packages."

"Marshal Stone, about my horses. You figuring to buy another for yourself?"

"No, sir. This one will be for a fellow by the name of Eutychus Bly. He's one of my deputies." Jubal said that to hide the fact that Bly was training to be a Kansas range detective. "Right now, he's riding shank's mare."

"I've got a couple of four-year-old's that might interest you. One's green broke, but the other is ready to go. All either of them need are some wet blankets. Either would fit the bill. And you know I would give you a lawman's rate."

"Does that rate go for judges also?"

"Judges?"

"Judge Brewster will be footing the bill for this one. Told me to tell you he'd be out to settle up with you soon."

Salice raised a finger. "Didn't know that getting a new horse comes with serving as a deputy to a United States Marshal. I might put in to be one of your deputies myself."

"Well, it doesn't, really. I'll explain to you fellows later."

Maddie picked up on what Jubal was saying and knew he

meant he'd tell her pa and Salice what was on his mind when she wasn't present.

"I'm going to fetch the eggs and feed the chickens." She pointed at Salice. "Don't forget that we're going riding."

Salice smiled. "I haven't forgotten." Then he looked to Jubal who was staring at him. "What are you looking at, Jubal?"

"I believe I'm looking at a fellow smitten, as they say, with a certain young lady."

Hiram listened for Salice's response, although it wasn't necessary. He knew that Maddie and Salice were in love. It reminded him of his sparking days with Maria, Maddie's ma.

"Marshal, since Maddie and Salice will be riding the colts, you can get a better look at them. I'll fetch them up from the pasture."

Jubal nodded as Hiram turned to get a bucket of feed. Salice stepped over and said, "Who's this Eutychus Bly?"

"Eutychus Bly is a fellow from Kansas that we've been training up to be a range detective."

"Kansas. He's a fer piece from home."

"Yeah, I got roped into this by Judge Brewster. Governor Hoppe of Kansas actually was the one that pulled the strings on this."

"The governor of Kansas." Salice whistled. "The big hog at the trough."

Salice didn't know how accurate he was in describing Hoppe. He was a big man and from the big belly that hung over his belt, it was obvious he stayed at the trough regularly.

"Yeah. He pulled the wool over our eyes. Asked me to train three men to be special range detectives but ended up sending the Bly family—a man, a woman, and a twelve-year-old boy." Jubal chuckled. "But I tell you what, now I'm glad he did. A finer family you haven't met. Speaking of family, how's your ma?"

"She's doing well. Loves Arlington. Has her a job at one of the diners."

"That's swell, Salice. Say, how long you going to be here?"

"Two more days. Had some papers I had to deliver to Abilene and figured I'd stop off and say howdy to Maddie."

"Well, brother, if I remember correctly, Waco's not exactly on your way back home to Arlington."

"Is that right? Reckon I got a little off on my directions."

"Salice Sanchez gettin' lost? Now I've heard it all. How about you and Maddie coming for supper tomorrow night? We'll invite the Blys as well. I'd like for you to meet Eutychus."

"All right. How's my little nephew Monty doing?"

"Growing like a weed."

Hiram came walking back into the barn leading two colts. One of them was the spitting image of Powder, which made sense given the gelding was sired by the same stallion and birthed by the same broodmare. The other colt was about the same size but a different color, more reddish than grey. It put Jubal in mind of his big red roan.

"Mr. Skinner," said Jubal as he stepped closer and looked the horses over, "both of them are dandies."

"Obliged, Marshal. Maddie's been riding the blue roan quite a bit in the last month. Does he look a little familiar to you?"

Jubal nodded. "He's Powder right down to his hooves. He's the one, Hiram, but I have a favor to ask Salice."

"What's that, Jubal?" asked Salice with a grin.

"Before you leave back for Arlington, you reckon you could teach Blue yonder to lie down like your pinto does?"

Salice compressed his lips and pushed up on the brim of his hat. "I could give it a try. He's young but not too young to learn a trick or two. Why do you want him to lie down?"

Jubal sighed. "Out on them Kansas Plains, Eutychus is going to need to be able to disappear at the drop of a hat. There ain't much cover in that part of the country."

"I'll see what I can do... Brother."

After brushing down Blue, Hiram dragged a saddle and blanket from the tack room. Salice quickly stepped over and took it from him.

"Let me get that, Mr. Skinner."

Skinner released the tack into Salice's hands then looked back to Jubal and pointed. "I done told him to call me Hiram but looks like he's set on Mr. Skinner." Hiram flashed a slight frown at Salice, but in reality appreciated the respect Sanchez showed him.

Blue shifted around a bit as Salice lifted the blanket then the saddle. He was built like his full brother, Powder, just a mite bigger in the chest and his legs were a darker black. Jubal knew he had secured a fine horse for Eutychus Bly.

Maddie came skipping back to the barn a few minutes later then she and Salice climbed aboard the colts and rode them around as Jubal and Hiram watched. Maddie had Blue cantering in a circle with his head low. It looked like she was sitting in a rocking chair, moving with the stride of the roan. Then she touched his belly with her boots and he took off like a bullet.

"Yeah, that Blue is a mover." Jubal stared back at Powder tethered to the hitch. He whinnied. His ears pitched forward as he bent his neck to the right and watched intently the pair of horses racing across the flats, looking as if he wanted to join the frolic. "If he's half the horse as that one yonder, Bly will have all he needs under saddle."

"Bly?" said Hiram. "You talkin' about Eutychus Bly, the fellow I met in town the other day?"

"That's him, Hiram. He'll be headed back to Kansas soon as a lawman."

"You don't say? Well, I wish him the best of luck. But I know one thing. He'll be astraddle a game horse."

The moment Hiram said that, a question shot across Jubal's mind: *Does Eutychus even know how to ride a horse? I don't rightly know.* Searching for the answer to that question in his mind, he remembered how he'd promised to teach Del to ride. Maybe it was time he taught both Blys to ride.

"Hiram, I'll be back for Blue in a couple of days. The judge will be out to see you soon to settle up."

Skinner waved a hand, "Ain't no need for that, Jubal. I know that man's busier than the town gossip sitting on the bench at Riker's Mercantile dipping her snuff."

"And who would that be, Hiram?" smiled Jubal as if he didn't know.

"Well, I ain't calling names"—Hiram raised his hand to the sun—"but by now she's done sent some juicy tidbits out across her grapevine. You may be the topic today or maybe me, who knows?"

"Could be," said Jubal as he looked back to Salice and Maddie riding over a ridge on the colts. "But I've heard it said that it's when they stop talking about you that you should get to worrying."

Hiram patted his leg and pointed at Jubal and said, "I believe you're right about that, Marshal. But this little lady I'm referring to, she don't ever stop talking about nobody."

"You wouldn't be pointing your stick at that sweet little lady, Mrs. Hadley, now would you?"

"As I said, Marshal, I ain't calling names. It's not healthy to do so."

Jubal smiled, then walked toward Powder. Untying him, he swung up in the saddle and touched his hat. "Good day, Hiram. Be out in a couple of days for Blue."

8

Jubal rode back into town and spoke with F.M. about the progress Eutychus was making with his pistol.

"Well, he can sure get to it quick now and ain't half bad about hitting what he points out. Of course, that shouldn't be no surprise given who's teaching him."

Jubal shook his head at F.M.'s embellishment, although she was right. But Jubal was not about to agree with her.

"He's gotten right handy with a Winchester as well, he and Del."

"Jubal, I was meaning to ask you about Del. How does he fit into all of this? I mean, he's twelve years old for goodness' sake. Surely he ain't going to be a lawman in Kansas at his age."

"No, he's not, F.M." Jubal rubbed the back of his neck. "I have to admit it's bothered me a bit, working with Del. I wouldn't put that boy in danger for nothing, but him knowing how to handle that rifle just might keep him and his folks alive should them landgrabbers come calling again."

Miller compressed her lips and went toward the coffee pot. "You might be right, Jubal. I can't imagine what the Blys have been through." As she poured her coffee, she took a sip and said, "But they ain't the same folks that left Kansas as they are now. Your Nancy's been working with Myra on the shotgun."

"What?" said Jubal incredulously.

"Sure enough. She told Myra that being able to use her shotgun kept a bad man from doing bad things to her and her family."

Jubal nodded and smiled. "Dang if I didn't marry myself a frontier woman. She's a wildcat. Reminds me of somebody else I know." Jubal's eyes darted to F.M.

"Nancy Stone's as fine as they come. A real lady, but a lady who don't put up with nobody messing with her family. I believe her words were just what Myra Bly needed to hear. She had been a little skittish of that shotgun until then. After Nancy's talk, she grabbed up the gun and walloped that target out in front of her."

Jubal had wondered where Myra was going to fit in to all of this. Now, he was relieved to hear that she, too, was willing to learn how to defend herself, even if it meant taking the life of her aggressor.

The next few moments Jubal and F.M. both seemed to be lost in thought. Neither said anything as they both sipped their coffee. Jubal walked to the window and looked up and down the street. Everything was calm, just the way he liked it. Then there was a tap on the door.

"Come on in," said Jubal as he took another gulp of coffee.

It was young Danny Ferguson, one of the runners for the telegraph office.

89

"Marshal, you got a wire from Deputy Burns." He held the piece of paper out for Jubal to take.

"Thank you, Danny." Jubal pulled a nickel from his vest pocket and tossed it in the air. Danny caught it and grinned from ear to ear.

"Obliged, Marshal. I best get back. Might be other wires I need to deliver." He looked to F.M. "Deputy Miller, you sure look pretty today, ma'am."

Miller smiled at the boy then caught Jubal's stare. "Well, thank you Danny," she said as she walked to the door. "Glad there's at least one man in Waco who knows a pretty lady when he sees one."

"Where, where?" smiled Jubal as he looked to his left and right. Danny chuckled as F.M. rolled her eyes. Then he stepped out on the stoop and pulled the door shut.

Jubal commenced to reading the telegram. Then he shook his head and brushed his hand against the paper.

"Well, Tanner's to stay another week in Burnett."

F.M. stared across the room at Jubal. He caught her gaze then lifted a hand. "I know, F.M. You don't have to tell me how Tanner not being here—"

"Nah, Jubal. I wasn't going to say that." She walked to the window and peeked out. "Have you thought about asking Euty-chus to do a little deputying for you?"

Jubal's head jerked backwards. Miller took that as resistance to her suggestion but continued her line of thought.

"He needs the experience and we done about taught him all we can. Now it's time for him to be tested, don't you think?"

Jubal slammed his hand down on his desk. Miller frowned. Then Jubal smiled as he took a sip of his coffee. "Dang if you don't have something there, Miller. I just hate it that I didn't think of it."

"Want me to fetch him, Jubal? Me and Razor can be back in three shakes of a lamb's tail."

"First things first, F.M."

"What do you mean by that?"

"I went out to Hiram Skinner's ranch today and picked out a horse for Eutychus. A blue roan, Powder's full brother."

"Well, I don't reckon there's a better place you could have found one than Hiram's. He raises some good ones. Of course, not the quality of Razor but some good horses nonetheless."

"Yeah," chuckled Jubal. Then he continued, "Now all we have to do is teach Eutychus to ride." Jubal stared a hole in F.M.

She raised a hand. "Now wait just a blame minute. I done taught him about guns. Horses, well, that'll have to be someone else. I can't think of anybody better than you, Jubal."

Sighing deeply, Jubal set down his cup and shuffled around the papers on his desk. Then he slowly looked over at Miller.

"So, you think we ought to pin a deputy badge on Bly?"

"Yes, sir, I do. I'm anxious to see how he uses what we've taught him."

"All right. Let's go," Jubal said as he stood and walked toward the door. Lifting his hat, he said, "I'm not sure Powder can keep up with that powerful steed you were talking about earlier."

Miller smiled. "I'll keep a tight rein on Razor to give your roan a chance."

When they arrived at the Dawsons' farm where the Blys were staying, Jubal and F.M. swung down and quickly heard gunshots behind the barn. They figured Eutychus was honing his skills with his Colt.

"Let's slip around there and take a look," said Jubal. As they did, they were both pleased to see how proficient Eutychus was with the use of his Colt. Then he spun on his heels and raised the gun toward them.

"I thought I felt somebody behind me," he smiled.

Jubal and F.M. stepped out from the corner of the barn with their hands up and smiling.

"Don't shoot," said Jubal.

Eutychus spun his pistol on his finger and put the Colt back into the holster. It looked like he'd been doing that all his life. Then he walked toward them as he looked back at the target.

Humbly he said, "I'm hittin' the target now more times that I'm missing, Deputy Miller, thanks to you."

"I can see that, Eutychus," said F.M. "I'm plumb proud of you. Dang, the way you're plugging that bullseye, the marshal here just might offer you a job."

"A job?" Bly asked as he opened the chambers and pulled out the spent cartridges, replacing them with new ones. It was obvious to Jubal and F.M. that Eutychus Bly was a different man since arriving in Waco. He had a confidence about him that was very obvious to both peace officers.

"Deputy Burns has been delayed in Burnett."

"That's the town that was infested with highbinders, wasn't it, Marshal. That town you and them other lawmen cleaned up?"

"Yes, sir. That's the one. Burns is going to be there another week. That's makes me a little shy on deputies. What would you say to pinning on a deputy marshal's badge for a spell?"

Eutychus looked up at Jubal, stunned by his request.

"You want me to be one of your deputies, Marshal? I mean... am I ready for that assignment?"

"I do, and you are," answered Stone flatly. "Now, there is one more skill you need to learn before you head back to Kansas, but it won't keep you from wearing a badge."

"I'd be honored to serve as your deputy, Marshal Stone."

"Good."

"Marshal, what was that other skill you said I needed to learn?"

"Equitation."

"What's that?" asked Eutychus.

Miller chuckled and answered, "Learning to ride and shoot off of a horse."

Eutychus' eyes widened. "I've been astraddle many a mule but only a couple of horses."

Del was now standing at the corner of the building. He stepped out and said, "Pa, we can learn together."

Jubal turned on his boot heels and pointed. "That's a good idea, Del. Seems to me I promised you a ride aboard Red."

"Yes, sir, you did. But Pa..." Del looked at Eutychus then looked down to the ground.

Eutychus chuckled. "That's all he's been talking about for the last couple of weeks, Marshal. We didn't want him to bother you."

"Ain't no bother. Del, how about you go open that corral and I'll bring Powder over. Would you settle for riding him today instead of Red?"

Del's mouth flung open. He took off like a bullet and did as Jubal said. A few minutes later, he was in the saddle, riding Powder in the enclosure. Jubal gave him some directions on how to handle the reins and keep his weight in the stirrups, even though they were a little long for him. Eutychus listened and watched.

After about eight times around the corral, Del brought the roan to a stop by the gate. Leaning forward in the saddle, he patted Powder on the neck then looked toward Eutychus. "Pa, you figure one day we'll have a horse like this?"

Eutychus smiled. "He's a fine animal, Del. A mite better than ol' Bessie, our mule."

Jubal had his arms draped over the rails. He looked over at F.M. She smiled back. They both knew that soon the Blys would indeed have a horse like Powder, almost the spitting image of the blue roan.

"All right, Eutychus. It's your turn. Del, step down and let your pa have a go," smiled Jubal. "Climb aboard, Mr. Bly." He motioned with his head toward Powder.

With some hesitation, Eutychus opened the corral gate. Del came out and he went in. Then he reached and grabbed the reins and saddle horn and pulled himself up. He was about the same height as Jubal, so the stirrups seemed to fit him well.

He picked up the reins and Powder moved forward. Jubal told him to sift around in his saddle and get square over the horse's withers. As he did, he mistakenly nudged the gelding in the belly. Powder broke into a run, dumping Eutychus off the back.

Jubal quickly crawled between the lodge poles and raced to Eutychus to make sure he was okay and to keep Powder from running over him.

"You all right?" Jubal asked him as he kneeled down over him and held up his hand toward the horse to stop him.

Eutychus smiled. "Reckon I wasn't expecting that, but I've always heard if you get thrown off a horse, get right back on."

Jubal pulled him to his feet. Eutychus walked straight over to Powder and eased up to him, speaking softly. Jubal wanted to help him but knew Bly needed to do this by himself. He reached up and grabbed the saddle horn and pulled himself up. Gathering his reins, he shifted from side to side but careful not to put his heels to the roan's side as he did earlier. Making six or eight more loops around the corral, he pulled the gelding to a stop, patted him on the neck, and dismounted.

"Hope one day I'll have a horse like you, ol' boy. You're a lot of animal, you are."

Jubal smiled again, knowing that soon he'd be riding back out to Hiram Skinner's ranch to fetch Blue.

9

"Del, Fetch Powder out of the corral. Deputy Miller and I need to get back to town." Jubal opened the gate then he looked at Eutychus. "You'll begin deputying Friday morning. That'll give you a couple of days to catch up on things around here."

"Pa, you're going to be a deputy marshal?" Del asked Eutychus with a smile as big as Texas as he handed Jubal Powder's leather reins.

"Yeah, son. You reckon I can pull my freight?"

"Yes, sir, and then some," Del answered. Then he looked to Jubal, "Don't you think so, Marshal Stone?"

Jubal winked. "You bet, Del. I only hire the best deputies on the frontier."

"Well, thank you, Jubal," said F.M. with a crooked grin as she climbed up on Razor and spat.

Jubal stuffed his boot in his stirrup and mounted Powder. Gathering his reins, he shook his head. "'Course, I have been known to make a mistake or two choosing the right deputies, one in particular."

Miller looked to Eutychus and Del and pursed her lips. "He's just sore 'cause me and Razor bested him and that buzzard bait on our way out here."

"Deputy Miller, I hope you're figuring to go to church Sunday morning, telling them kind of blanket stretchers and all. Parson Willis may need to have a talk with you."

"I'm going to say howdy to Myra, Jubal. By then you'll be finished with your sermon." She bumped Razor with her spurs and trotted off.

"Del, you best get on with your chores, son. I need to speak to the marshal."

"Yes, sir, Pa. Thanks for letting me ride your horse, Marshal Stone."

"You bet, son." Jubal raised a finger to his hat. Del went into the barn to feed and milk the cow.

"Marshal Stone," Eutychus said as he looked back to see Del disappear into the barn. "You reckon I'm ready for deputying, sure enough?"

"We'll find out soon enough, Eutychus, but... my money is on you, my friend."

Jubal began to ride away when he stopped and wheeled Powder around. "F.M. thinks you're ready, and that's good enough for me. You handle deputying like you do that Colt and you'll do fine. See you directly."

Three days later, Jubal came back out to see Eutychus. This time he was riding Red and leading Blue, the horse he had secured from Hiram Skinner. A new saddle was on his back. As he rode up, Eutychus was out at the barn, putting an edge on an axe. Del was spreading fresh straw on the barn floor.

"Hello in the barn!" Jubal called out.

Del leaned his pitchfork against the wall and darted to the door.

"It's Marshal Stone, Pa, and looks like he's brought Powder back out for you to ride."

"Well," said Eutychus, "let's go say good morning." He laid his axe beside the grinding wheel and wiped his hands on his pants as he walked out.

"Howdy, Marshal Stone," said Del with a big smile on his face. He went straight to Red and rubbed his muzzle.

"Good morning, gents," said Jubal. "All right if I step down?"

"Jubal, you know you're welcome anytime. You don't have to ask."

"But others should, Eutychus. Here on the frontier, it's just an understanding that a visitor waits to be asked to step down. And if he jumps down out of his saddle before, you put him right back in it."

Eutychus nodded. "Will do."

Del was listening. He always listened when Jubal spoke. He knew the marshal's directives were important for his father and himself.

"Is it all right if I step down?"

"Yes, Marshal. You are welcome. I see you brought Powder back out today. Reckon it's time for my next riding lesson."

"Well, you're half right, Eutychus." Jubal pointed back at Blue. "This ain't Powder. His name is Blue, and he's yourn, along with the tack."

Eutychus' head jerked backward as did Del's.

"Do you mind repeating that, Marshal? I've had that grinding wheel spinning this morning and I believe it's affected my hearing." He tugged at his ear.

Jubal smiled. "Sure, Eutychus. This here is Blue. He's a full-blooded brother to Powder and one of Mr. Skinner's colts. He's yourn along with the tack. You'll need him in Kansas."

Tears welled up in Eutychus' eyes as in Del's. Myra came walking toward the barn and waved a hand. Then she saw her husband and son's tears and thought the worst.

"What's wrong, Eutychus?" She looked to her husband then down to Del. "Del?"

Del stepped over to Myra and smiled up at her. "Ain't nothing wrong, Ma. Marshal Stone just told Pa this here horse and tack belong to him now."

Myra put her hand to her mouth. Now her eyes were filling with tears, tears of joy, tears of appreciation.

Jubal raised a hand. "Now, I ain't the one who bought the horse for you, Eutychus, but I did pick him out. He's a dandy. Fast as a cat and strong as a pair of oxen. He'll take you where you need to go and bring you back."

"I don't know what to say, Jubal."

"Don't say nothing. Just climb in the saddle. Del, you ride along with your pa on Red."

Both Eutychus and Del stepped forward and took the reins to each horse. Then they started to climb up when Jubal offered a warning: "Don't ever trust another man to saddle your horse. Always check your cinch and backstrap before mounting."

Eutychus and Del nodded and did as the marshal said. Then they both climbed aboard and rode around the homestead.

"Marshal Stone," said Myra as she stepped closer to him,

"you just don't know what it's meant to Eutychus and Del for you to—"

"Mrs. Bly," Jubal politely interrupted as he pushed up on the brim of his hat, "the pleasure has been mine. Don't know that I've ever met a family more deserving than yours. You folks have been through a lot of hard times and came out standing on your feet. You've already earned the respect of the folks of Waco."

"We're obliged. You and your town have been good to us."

"Well, ma'am," Jubal said, kicking the dirt with his boot, "you folks are easy to be good to."

"Marshal"—Myra's tone changed from grateful to serious—"I want to ask you something."

"Do I think Eutychus Bly can do the job of a range detective?" interjected Jubal.

She chuckled. "How did you know I was going to ask you that?"

"Because I reckon I've asked myself that question a dozen times since I met Eutychus. And with every week, I've seen him work harder and harder to master the gun and the other skills we've been teaching him. Eutychus has the drive. Now he needs the confidence and that's where we all come in."

Jubal turned to face Myra and said, "You know what me keeps going besides the Good Lord? Nancy, that wife of mine. She believes me and tells me that often. Do you believe in Eutychus, Myra?"

"Yes, I certainly do."

"Then tell him that often." Jubal looked back toward Eutychus and Del. "They're doing fine. That Del is a fine young man. I hope little Monty will be like him."

Myra smiled. Her love for her son was strong. "Obliged for you saying so, Marshal."

Jubal turned to Myra and said, "Now, I ain't going to sugarcoat the truth, Mrs. Myra. Being a frontier lawman is dangerous. It can get you killed and your family killed. My pa was the sheriff of Abilene when four men rode out to our place and gunned him down, along with my ma and sister."

Jubal looked over at Myra to make sure he wasn't overwhelming her. Ironically, she was nodding as if she'd heard this story before. She looked as if she wanted to say something so Jubal waited.

"Nancy told me about that, Marshal. I hope you don't mind."

"No, ma'am, I don't. I haven't shared that in a long time, but I just thought you needed to know the risks involved before setting back out for Kansas."

Jubal looked back at Eutychus and Del. "Looks like both Bly men were rooted in the saddle from birth. That Del sure loves horses."

"He sure does. I reckon he gets that from me."

"From you, Mrs. Bly?" Jubal asked incredulously as he looked back at her.

"My father had some riding stock. He had me in the saddle when I was three years old."

Jubal put his fingers to his mouth and whistled. Eutychus and Del came trotting back toward the barn. When they stopped, Jubal said, "Myra wants to ride."

Myra raised a hand in protest and took a step back toward the house. "No, I..."

"Mrs. Bly," said Jubal in a low tone, "I need to know how well you can ride."

Myra nodded as Del climbed down off Red.

"Here, Ma. Come ride Red. He'll take good care of you."

Myra checked the cinch, which impressed Jubal, then she grabbed the slack in the latigo strap hanging down and pulled herself up. Gathering the reins, she looked over at Eutychus. "You want to ride with me, Mr. Bly?" she asked with a warm smile.

Eutychus looked down at Jubal and Del and said, "I never pass up an opportunity to ride with a pretty lady." Then the two of them rode off.

"I never knew Ma could ride a horse," said Del as he grinned with satisfaction. The way she sat the saddle, Jubal could tell she was a skilled rider. Myra moved with Red as if they were one.

"Del, I figure there's a lot of things your ma can do that you don't know about yet. These frontier women are a rare breed. They don't brag about what they can do; they just do it."

When Myra and Eutychus came back, Jubal said, "I'll meet you at the forks in the morning at daybreak, Eutychus. Drovers will be in town tomorrow night, and I figure that will be a good time to get your feet wet deputying."

Eutychus nodded and said, "I'll be there, Marshal."

As Jubal began to ride away, he stopped and wheeled Red back around. "Leave the Winchester here. I've got one in the office for you. Never know when Myra or Del will have to shoot a bandit or a highbinder out here."

Eutychus smiled as he put his arm around Myra. Then he led Blue into the barn to strip his gear, rub him down, and get better acquainted with his new mount.

10

───────────

When the rooster crowed on the Blys' homestead, Eutychus was already riding for the forks aboard Blue. The roan was frisky and crow-hopped several times as Eutychus rode him down the lane and out to the main road. Del watched from his window with pride. He had seen his father master the skill of sidearms and the rifle. Now Eutychus was directing an eleven-hundred-pound animal with one hand. Del couldn't have been prouder of his father. To boot, he knew his pa was on his way to serve his first day as a United States Deputy Marshal.

Eutychus arrived at the forks early. Blue whinnied and his ears perked to the right. Eutychus stepped down and rubbed the roan's forehead. The horse nuzzled him, pushing him forward.

"He seems to like you," came a voice in the dawn. It was Jubal sitting atop Powder behind a small gnarled live oak. They rode forward out of cover.

"I didn't even know you were there, Marshal."

"Yeah, but your horse did."

"My horse?"

"Did you hear him whinny and see him look to the right?"

Eutychus frowned and shook his head. "No, I don't reckon I did."

"Deputy Bly, you always need to know your surroundings. Watch your horse. His senses are much better than yours or mine. When they throw their head or pitch their ears forward or whinny, be ready for whatever. My horses have saved my bacon many times."

Eutychus nodded. Jubal could tell his new deputy was dispirited by his ignorance. He was trying so hard, but like the young horse he was riding, Eutychus needed some wet blankets, some experience. He was about to get it in Waco.

As they got about a mile from town, Jubal turned off the road and toward an opening. Blue followed Powder track for track without Eutychus moving the reins. Jubal suddenly stopped and put his hands atop his horn. Eutychus pulled up beside him.

"Something wrong, Marshal?" he asked as he dropped his hand to his pistol.

"Yes, sir, there is. There's some rough-lookin' fellers coming our way. I believe it's Black Jack Beeson and his boys. Remember, you've been after them for two weeks now?"

Eutychus stared at Jubal for a moment then realized the marshal was teaching him another lesson so he played along.

"Yep. Black Jack Beeson and his boys. Sure looks like them to me."

Jubal swiveled in his saddle and looked behind him. Then he looked to his left then to his right.

"The problem is, Deputy Bly, if they see you, they'll shoot

you on sight. And out here, there's nowhere to hide. What are you going to do? They'll see you and your horse for sure out here in the open."

Eutychus sighed. "I reckon I'd snatch my rifle and belly up on the ground."

"What about your horse? Wouldn't they see him?"

Eutychus stared down at Blue. Scratching at his chin, he tried to think of a solution, but nothing came to him. "I don't rightly know, Marshal. What would you do in that situation?"

"Well, if I was riding Blue yonder," he gestured with his head to Eutychus' horse, "I'd tap him behind the left shoulder with the tip of my boot and pull back on his right rein."

Eutychus stared at Jubal for a moment then nudged Blue behind the shoulder with the tip of his boot and pulled back on the right rein. The roan gathered his weight up under him, bent his front legs, and went down on his belly. Eutychus stepped off as he did and stared in disbelief.

"Now, get down beside him and lay your rifle over the saddle."

Eutychus, again, did as the marshal told him.

"I believe that'll work. Stand astraddle him, yank on his rein, and cluck to him. He should stand."

Eutychus did as Jubal said, and the roan climbed to his feet with Eutychus in the saddle. Bly was dumbfounded. First, he's given one of the finest riding horses he'd ever seen with a new saddle. Now he'd learned that the horse will lie down on his command.

"Jubal, did you teach Blue to do that?"

"Nah, my brother Salice did."

"I'm obliged. That beats all I ever saw."

"I figured you'd need cover on the Kansas Plains, especially where there's no trees."

"That I will. That I will," he said as he patted the gelding on the neck.

"Let's get into town. Tonight we're going to have our hands full. Claude Tillman's bringing his cattle in to be railed from Waco to Fort Worth. When his cowboys get them cows in the corral, they're going to cut the wolf loose."

"You expecting trouble, Marshal?"

"Yep, and plenty of it. Two years ago when they came through, they busted out every window on Main Street and wrecked a couple of saloons. You ready to see what that hoss can do?"

Eutychus tightened up on his reins and got square over Blue's withers. Sinking his boots in his belly, the horse leaped forward in a run toward town. Jubal saw lots of daylight between Eutychus britches and the saddle he was in and out of as the blue roan chewed up the ground.

Red matched Blue stride for stride. Jubal looked over at Eutychus and said, "Give him some rein and let him run."

Eutychus pushed the reins up on his neck and Blue seemed to catch another gear. Now Jubal was running full chisel to catch him. When they got to where the road widened, Jubal hollered, "Pull up, Eutychus."

Eutychus slowed the roan to a gallop then to a trot. Blue was dancing in place sideways, wanting to run some more. Red was doing the same.

"What do you think about that pile of bones there, Eutychus? Reckon he could run down a highbinder trying to evade the law?"

"You bet he could, Marshal," said Eutychus with a proud

grin on his face as he held a tight rein and stroked Blue's mane. "He's faster than a bullet. There were a couple of times back yonder I thought I was going to leave the saddle."

"But you didn't, Eutychus. Just keep your weight in your stirrups and stay square over his withers, just like you were doing."

"I ain't never ridden anything as fast as Blue."

"He can cover some ground, all right." Jubal pointed to Blue. "Just take care of him, and he'll take care of you. He's a young horse and bred to run. He's got a lot to learn yet."

"Sounds like somebody else I know," smiled Eutychus as they continued toward town.

Jubal nodded. "You ready to pin on a badge and get your feet wet at being a lawman?"

"By jingo, I believe I am. What else do I need to know about Mr. Tillman and his men?"

"Claude's a bear when he's mad. He don't like the law or lawmen. You see, he and his family have been in these parts for several generations now. There wasn't any law when they came. They just kind of had their own code."

"So, when he comes to town he just does as he pleases, Marshal?"

"To a point. I've thrown him in jail before. He didn't like it nary a bit. Fact is, he doesn't like it none when we arrest his men for breaking the law either. Of course, the remedy for that is, they behave themselves."

"He sounds like a mean one. Reminds me of a few fellows in Kansas. They thought they owned the whole world. Acted like nobody else mattered."

"Then you've met Claude Tillman," said Jubal.

"Yeah, I've met Claude Tillman," Eutychus said with a snarl.

Jubal liked Eutychus' moxie. He would need it if he was

going to survive as a frontier lawman, whether range detective or deputy.

As they rode into town, Jubal whistled as they passed the blacksmith's shop. Curly Snipes came out holding a tong with a horseshoe glowing red at the end.

"Be right there, Marshal."

Eutychus nodded at Curly and continued to ride alongside Jubal. Today he wasn't in Waco as a citizen. He was here on business, lawman's business. In a few minutes, Eutychus knew that Jubal was going to pin a badge to his shirt and swear him in. He was a little overwhelmed with that notion but at the same time so excited he could hardly keep a smile off his face. To boot, he was astraddle a horse that looked exactly like Stone's. A fine horse that any man would be honored to own and ride.

Pulling up at the jail hitch, Jubal swung down and tied off Powder. Eutychus did the same with Blue. As they climbed the steps, they both saw Curly coming their way.

"You met Mr. Snipes, haven't you, Eutychus?"

"Yes, I have."

"He's another of my deputies. Just his size makes most folks around here think twice before doing something stupid. He don't like Tillman's men coming to town. Their last visit, they used one of the walls of his shop for target practice. He boogered up a three of them cowboys before five more of them piled on."

"Marshal, you got some coffee on the boil? I sure could use another cup," said Snipes as he got closer, toting a pair of hand irons.

"If I know F.M. Miller, there's some on the other side of this door. I see you got my hand irons."

"Yes, sir, and I can hammer out more if you need me to."

Jubal turned the doorknob and walked right into the steel sights of a Winchester Miller had raised and was cleaning, the last of six she had already oiled. The moment she heard that Tillman and his rowdies were coming to town, she started preparing for their arrival.

"State your business, gents, and do it quickly," Miller said with a smile as she held the rifle on the three men.

Jubal shook his head and stepped on inside.

"Howdy, Miss F.M.," said Curly as he pulled off his hat and grinned. He was sweet on Miller and had been for some time, although she didn't feel the same way about him.

F.M. rolled her eyes and said, "Mr. Snipes."

Jubal chuckled as he headed for the coffee pot. Speaking over his shoulder, he said to Miller, "F.M., reach yonder in that drawer and fetch out two deputy badges."

Miller laid the rifle over the desk and pulled open the drawer. Fingering the badges, she stared down at them then up to Eutychus. "Mr. Bly, you ready to wear one of these?"

"I am," Eutychus said with a confidence that days ago was lacking.

Curly stepped forward and made his request. "Miss F.M., would you pin mine on for me? You know, with these big fingers"—he held up his big palms, revealing hands the size of a grizzly bear's paws—"I'm all thumbs."

She nodded, stood to her feet, and waved him forward.

Again, Jubal chuckled as he sipped his coffee and looked out the window. He knew that the blacksmith was sweet on F.M. and that it bothered his deputy.

Curly tipped his head at F.M. "Obliged.

Jubal looked across the room at Bly. "Eutychus, come on

over here and get you a cup of coffee while F.M. pins on Curly's badge."

Miller caught the sarcasm in Jubal's voice and tossed him a stern glare. Curly stepped forward and leaned down.

Standing to her feet and reaching up, she affixed the badge to Snipes' shirt then held up Eutychus'. "You ready?"

"Yes, ma'am." Eutychus came over, carrying his cup of coffee. Setting it down on the desk, he stepped forward.

"All right, Marshal, I believe Mr. Bly is ready to take the oath along with Curly," said Miller.

Jubal told them both to raise their right hands and repeat after him. After both men took the oath, Stone told everybody to take a seat. Miller stepped aside to give Jubal his chair as she lifted the Winchester from the desk and stepped over to put it back in the cradle.

"Let's talk about this afternoon and tonight when Tillman's men hit town," said Jubal as he took another gulp of coffee. "Dang, that Arbuckle's is good. Reckon the judge delivered on his promise."

Miller smiled. "Yep. Mr. Riker dropped a fresh bag off this morning."

"All right, let's get down to business. I got word that Tillman's boys might be running some stolen cattle on this drive. Sheriff Henry Bowers of McGregor said his deputy spotted a small herd about two miles behind Tillman's bigger one. When they camped for the night, the drovers joined Tillman's bunch."

"You figure they'll mix them together before they load them on the train for Fort Worth, Jubal?" asked Miller.

"Yep, but they'll need a diversion first. They know we'll be watching the pens otherwise."

Jubal reached in his desk and pulled out a pencil and piece

of paper. "Now, Claude's brand is the Triple T." He drew it out on paper to show his deputies. "I'm going to get with Henry at the depot and tell him to give them steers a close look over before he loads them. I figure they'll run them all together just before they reach town. That's why I'm going to be watching from Jenkin's Rise."

"About that diversion you mentioned, Marshal," said Curly. "You mean like rowdies busting out windows down Main Street and putting holes in my shop, that kind of diversion?"

"Yep, that's right, Curly. That's why I wanted to have plenty of hand irons available. Those three cells will fill up fast, but we ain't going to stop arresting the misbehaving until we've got them all corralled."

"And Tillman, Jubal? What are your plans for him?" asked F.M.

"Well, if I can prove he's guilty of cattle rustling, he won't be going back home this time."

Jubal looked over at Eutychus. He knew his new deputy was nervous.

"F.M, I want you and Eutychus to be visible on the board-walks. Stay together. This being Eutychus' first day of deputy-ing, I don't want him dealing with Tillman's men alone."

"Right, Jubal," said F.M. When it came to dealing with keeping Waco safe, nobody took it more seriously, other than the marshal.

"Curly, I want you down by the loading pens. Any of them drovers give you a hard time, crack some skulls. I want them to know that if they choose to break the law, there will be dire consequences. From a broken window, to molesting citizens, to drunken disorder, the town of Waco won't tolerate any of it."

"How long will you be gone, Jubal?" asked Miller.

"I should be back to town before dark. Curly, I'll catch up with you at the corrals. Anybody have any questions?"

Eutychus looked a little overwhelmed. F.M. saw the concern on his face and said, "It'll be all right, Mr. Bly. This ain't our first rodeo," said Miller as she stood up and waved him over to the cradle of guns on the wall. "Choose your poison. All of them are clean and ready to dispense justice."

Eutychus pulled down the first one in the cradle, which was the last one F.M. had cleaned. "I'll take this one, I reckon."

"Let me see that smoke stick, Eutychus. Ain't sure I got all the oil off it." She held out her hand. He started to hand it to her but suddenly stopped.

"Can't let you have my rifle, ma'am."

F.M. smiled and looked across the room at Jubal. "He must have been taught by the best. Well done, Eutychus," Miller said as she smiled back at him.

11

"Eutychus, I reckon you ought to take Blue down to the livery and stall him," suggested Jubal.

"All right, Marshal," he said as he cradled the rifle in the bend of his arm. As he started for the door, he turned and said, "Deputy Miller, how would you like to lay eyes on one of the best horses Texas has ever seen?"

Miller chuckled and said, "You must be talking about Razor."

Eutychus shook his head. "No, ma'am, he's a fine one, but this one here is extra special." He pointed toward the door. "Come take a gander."

Jubal smiled. He enjoyed seeing the pride on Eutychus' face about his new blue roan. He motioned with his head for Miller to follow Bly.

As he pulled open the door, Blue threw his head toward him. "Yonder he is."

Miller followed him out on the stoop and said, "Dang if that don't look just like Powder."

Jubal was right behind them. "He should. He's the full brother to him."

Miller, too, enjoyed the look on Bly's face. He was beaming over his new horse.

Curly cleared his throat, looking over the shoulder of Jubal. "His first shoes are on me, Deputy Bly."

Eutychus looked back at Curly and said, "Obliged, Curly." He picked up Blue's head and said, "Did you hear what he called me, boy? Deputy Bly."

The enchanted moment was disturbed by the man who was riding by. F.M. looked back at Jubal and said, "You know who that is? Snake Jeffers."

"Snake Jeffers?" said Eutychus. "Is he one of Tillman's men?"

"Figure he is today," answered Jubal. "That's probably one of Claude's diversions we were talking about."

"Gunfighter, I'd say," said Curly as he stared a hole in the man riding down Main Street.

"Yes, sir. Don't have any posters out on him, but I figure I'll go say howdy before I ride out."

Jubal pulled on his hat and reached down to latch down the leather strap of his holster. When he started down the steps, he turned and looked to Eutychus. Pointing, he said, "You stay close to Deputy Miller. She'll show you the ropes." Jubal then looked to Curly. "Reckon you best get to the loading pens. I figure Tillman ain't fer behind."

As Jubal walked toward Jeffers, he couldn't help but worry a little about Eutychus. He knew firsthand how strong Eutychus was. A few weeks previous, when he suggested the former

Kansas sodbuster forget about becoming a range detective and just settle down in Texas and try his hand at farming, Eutychus lifted Stone off the ground in anger, expressing his determination to continue the training. But would Eutychus Bly have the toughness he needed to deal with men like Tillman and his cronies? Jubal didn't know the answer to that question, but soon would find out.

Stone walked to where he saw Jeffers stop and dismount. As the stranger was tying his horse to the hitching rail of the saloon, the marshal called his name.

"Snake Jeffers."

The gunman instinctively dropped his hand to his gun. Jubal already had his hovering over his Colt.

"What are you doing in Waco?"

"Just wetting my whistle, Marshal. That ain't against the law, now is it?" he asked with sarcasm in his voice.

"I don't like gun slicks in my town. Drink's on me. Then get."

Jeffers removed his hat and rubbed his face up and down. "I've had me a long ride today, Stone, and I ain't in the mood to be prodded so leave me be."

"Get your drink and move on. Or step out in the street yonder and we'll settle this now."

"You're a hard twist, aren't you, Stone? But... so am I."

Jeffers slowly climbed the steps and pushed through the short double saloon doors without looking back. Jubal headed to the livery to get Powder then he was off to surveil Tillman's operation. Jenkin's Rise was perched on the only road leading into Waco from the west, so Claude and his men would have to come right by where Jubal planned to set up.

It was getting the middle of the afternoon when Jubal

started hearing the lowing of cattle and saw a huge dust cloud off in the distance. He pulled his binoculars close to his eyes and glassed the drovers and cattle. It looked to be over a thousand head to him. It took two hours for the whole herd to pass by. As closely as he looked, he saw no brands other than the Triple T.

He waited for another half an hour before leaving his perch. Dusk was settling over the countryside when he climbed up in his saddle and headed back to town. When he reached the corrals, he immediately saw Curly walking the top boards overlooking the cattle. He also saw six of Tillman's men huddled up, the first rotation of nighthawks for the cattle. Since the corrals would only accommodate four hundred head, the rest would have to be bedded down nearby.

Jubal rode past Tillman's men without saying a word. That is until one of the drovers mouthed off.

"Well, if it ain't *Marshal Stone*," said the man as he wagged his head from side to side.

Stone wheeled his horse in a half circle to put an eyeball on the surly cowboy.

"I might have knowed it was you, Latigo. I know that big mouth of yours anywhere."

"Gentlemen"—the cowboy chuckled as he pointed—"I give you Jubal Stone, marshal extraordinaire, in the flesh." Latigo pulled off his hat and bowed.

"You're still a dang fool, I see." Jubal rode up closer to the man and stood in his saddle. Throwing his thumb toward the cattle, he said, "I reckon all them steers are wearing the Triple T brand, huh, Latigo?"

"Now, Marshal. You wouldn't be doubting our integrity, would you?"

"Latigo, I would if there was any integrity to doubt."

"A fellow could take offense to that, Stone," said the man sitting on the corral rails to the right of Latigo. He wore his gun low on his hip. "I don't like being called a liar, mister."

"Then you ought to be a little choosier with who you ride with, *mister*. What's your name?"

"Joe Tadlock. What's it to you?"

"Nothing. Absolutely nothing." Jubal spat.

The man started climbing down the rails, offended by Jubal's last statement. Latigo grabbed him by the arm and said, "Remember what Mr. Tillman said."

"And what would that be, Latigo?" asked Stone.

"Afraid that information is private, Marshal. Reckon I'll just have to leave you guessing."

"Boys," Stone said as he touched his hat with his hand. Then he rode toward Curly.

"I've got a mind to cut him down and be done with it," said Tadlock.

Latigo laughed, took a long drag on his cigarette, and said, "Boy, that fellow riding yonder has killed a passel of fools that thought they'd do the same. You face him, you best not do it alone."

Tadlock frowned. He thought himself to be better than a fair hand with his gun. Maybe this would be the time to prove it. He unlatched the leather loop over his hammer and took a step forward.

"Calm yourself, Tadlock," came an angry voice behind him. It was Claude Tillman aboard his palomino. "I told you, Latigo, to keep the boys in check. Ain't no need to get the marshal stirred up... yet."

"Yes, sir, Mr. Tillman." Latigo glared at Tadlock and said,

"Settle down, you dang fool, or you'll get us all fired or killed one day."

However, instead of Tadlock cooling off, he turned on his heels and said, "I'm not afraid of Jubal Stone... or anybody else for that matter, Mr. Tillman. He talks down to me again, and I'll—"

"You'll do nothing until I tell you to do something." Pointing down, Tillman continued, "You take my money, you wear my brand." He thumbed his chest. "That means I'm calling the shots, not some whelp still wet behind the ears."

Tadlock just stared up at his boss as if he was frozen. Was he ready to pull in his horns or yank iron on Tillman?

He slowly relaxed his stance and stared off in the distance. Tillman chuckled as he rode off. Looking over his shoulder, he said to his second in command, Bart Evans, "That fool reminds me of me when I was his age. We may ought to go ahead and pay him. If he's on the prod with Stone, he might not be around payday."

"In that case," smiled Evans, "let's just wait a spell. We might not have to pay him at all."

"Dang you, Bart," said Tillman with a grin as he leaned over and elbowed his foreman. "You've got a good head on your shoulders." But his grin quickly disappeared when he saw Stone up ahead talking to Curly.

"Somebody must have tipped him off. There ain't more than forty head in the herd wearing fresh brands, but Jubal Stone will find each and every one of them if he has half a chance."

"If we let him, boss," whispered Evans. "I figure he and his deputy will be up to their necks in trouble in just a bit. He won't have time to look too closely."

"That's right. That's right," answered Tillman as he swiveled in his seat, looking over the corral of steers. "Wonder if Jeffers has made it into town? Don't suppose I've met a man that hates lawmen as much as him... except for me."

For the next few minutes, Claude went on a rant about how he and his family settled a big part of Texas, how they fought Indians, ran off squatters, and had their own ways of justice, usually dispensed from the business end of a Winchester. Evans had heard this same story more times than he wanted to. But seeing that Tillman paid him good wages, he just nodded and acted as if this was the first time he'd heard of Claude's family history of settling the West.

Jubal and Curly spoke for a spell then both of them left to go back toward Main Street. They would be back at daybreak to check the brands.

Tillman licked his lips and said, "Let's go wet our whistle. Dang trail dust is sitting heavy in my throat."

"I'm with you, boss," said Evans as they both raised their horses to a trot.

Miller and Bly were moving up and down the boardwalks when three of Tillman's men started prodding them.

"Well, I heard Waco had a female deputy, but I didn't believe it. Lookie there, Ned. She has a badge and a gun. Reckon what I would have to do to get her attention?"

F.M. turned on her heels and said, "Just keep acting the giddy goat, mister, and you'll get my full attention."

"Elbert, I believe she's got you shaking in your boots. You better back down before she slaps iron on you."

Eutychus stared at the men then to F.M. He wasn't sure what to do next, but he didn't plan on listening much longer to this big mouth berate Miller.

"Now, Deputy, I don't want to get on your bad side. How

about you and me step into the saloon and ol' Elbert here will buy you a drink."

"No, thanks."

F.M. stepped around the man. As she did, he reached out and grabbed her arm. Miller met his action with her Colt drawn and pressed it into his gut.

"Don't you ever lay a hand to me, cowboy, or I'll fill your belly full of lead."

Elbert backed away, stunned by Miller's response. Then he folded his arms and chuckled. "Well, ain't you the wildcat? Lucky for you, I know how to tame wildcats." He stared back at the other drovers and winked. Then he turned and reached for her arm.

Eutychus stepped forward and grabbed hold of the man's arm and twisted it around his back. Then he slammed him up against the wall.

"You done worn out your welcome, cowboy. Now move along or go to jail."

Eutychus released him. The man went for his gun, but Bly was lightning fast. Shoving the Colt to his chin, he drew back the hammer.

Miller noticed a fire in Bly's eyes she had not seen before. His finger was slightly moving against the trigger.

"Deputy Bly. You warned him. I believe he'll behave himself now."

Eutychus released his arm and stepped back.

Elbert took a deep breath and rubbed his chin.

"Dang, you lawmen are a touchy sort. We were just having a little fun. No need to go heel."

Eutychus never broke his stare on the man, which made Elbert even more nervous.

Miller stepped between them and said, "Just move along, cowboy. No harm done."

As Elbert and his partners moved down the boardwalk, F.M. looked at Eutychus and asked, "Are you all right? Thought you were going to shoot 'im for a minute there."

Bly shook his head almost as if trying to erase the experience. Then he looked to Miller. "I'll never again tolerate a man being rude to a lady or... bucking the law."

Miller smiled. "Sounds like you been running with Jubal Stone."

Eutychus nodded. "Yes, ma'am. I've learned a lot from the marshal and from you, F.M., and I'm right grateful to you both."

Miller pointed. "Let's make another loop around town. It's getting dark and the spirits will be flowing freely here in a bit. That's when these drovers are going to show their colors."

Eutychus took a step then pointed. "Ain't that the marshal and Curly coming yonder?"

Miller strained her eyes to look to the far end of town. As the men got closer, she glanced over to her partner. "You got eagle's eyes, Eutychus, and to see them in the dark like that, well, that's... interesting."

Bly smiled. "I've always had good eyesight. I can see right well at long distances and pretty good at night."

"I believe you," she said as they walked toward Jubal and Curly.

As the law officers were walking toward each other, more of Tillman's riders rode by, six of them. Then Claude and his foreman, Evans, were on their drag. Claude pulled up as he got to Jubal.

"Marshal Stone, thought I'd let you know we made it into town. We'll be loading our cattle for Fort Worth in the morning.

Going to do my best to keep my boys in line while we're here, but you know how that is." Tillman chuckled as did Evans.

"Mr. Tillman." Jubal tipped his head. "You and your bunch are welcome in Waco... as long as you behave."

"Fair enough, Marshal. Fair enough." He smirked. Claude had a plan in mind to divert the marshal's attention from the corrals to the middle of town. It was just not late enough yet to put it into play.

As Tillman and his man rode away, F.M. stepped forward and said, "That ain't the same Tillman that came to town two years ago. That one yonder is as gentle as a lamb."

"Yeah, reminds me of some Bible verses my ma used to read us. Beware of wolves in sheep's clothing. Tillman has something up his sleeve. It was all over his face," said Jubal. "How are things up the street?" Stone looked to Miller and Bly.

"We had a little run-in with three of Tillman's men, but Eutychus here persuaded them to move along."

Jubal smiled. "Good. Good. Just keep walking the streets. Going to send Curly back to lock the livery cars. That way, we'll all be down at the depot in the morning looking over that herd. I find one steer with a fresh brand on it, I'm going to arrest Tillman. Now that I think about, I figure the last time he came through, he was up to this same stuff. We just didn't know about it. All them broken windows and busting up the saloons was to keep us from the loading pens."

12

Later that night, Tillman and his men began to execute their plan to stir up Waco. It started with a fight in the one of the saloons. Jubal heard F.M. whistle, and he and Curly came running.

Jubal sent Miller and Bly in the front as he slipped in from the back. Curly stayed on the boardwalk, watching the rooftops with a Winchester slung over his shoulder.

Then a shot rang out. It came from inside the saloon. Just as F.M. and Eutychus stepped through the front doors with drawn guns, they saw fire flare from the bore of a Colt. Holding the smoking gun was Joe Tadlock, the man Jubal had confronted earlier out at the stockyard.

"Drop that gun, Tadlock," Jubal ordered as he came in from the back.

"It was self-defense, Marshal, and nobody takes my gun." He put it back into his holster.

Jubal stepped forward and said, "Did anybody see what happened?"

Nobody answered for fear of retaliation.

Jubal turned back to Tadlock. "You're going to jail, Tadlock, until we can sort this out."

Joe crouched and said, "Told you nobody was taking my gun."

Off to the left, another of Tadlock's men lowered his hand to his holster. Eutychus caught his move and pointed across the room, "Mister, you go for that gun, and I'll kill you."

Because of her height, F.M. couldn't see the man Eutychus was talking to. He was behind another man.

Curly stepped to the swinging doors and peered over them, Winchester cocked and ready.

The man Eutychus warned raised his hands to the bar. Still Tadlock was crouched and ready to try his luck with Jubal.

"Now, I won't tell you again, Tadlock. Drop your gun and throw up your hands."

Tadlock went for his pistol but proved to be a hair too slow. Jubal's .44 barked and Tadlock went to his knees. The man Eutychus had warned earlier went for his gun. Bly snatched iron and sent a slug right into the man's chest. He yelled out as he spun around and grabbed for the bar. Then he fell to the floor, taking several mugs of beer with him.

All four lawmen now had their guns drawn as they studied the crowd. Nobody moved for fear of getting shot.

"You four men"—Jubal pointed down to Tadlock—"fetch him to the doc." Jubal stepped over to the man Eutychus had shot. "This one's done fer."

Eutychus stared at Jubal, doing his best to swallow down what he had just heard. He had killed a man that he was sure would have taken a shot at Marshal Stone. But still, the fact that he had just taken a man's life had his heart racing. Regret filled his eyes as he stared down at the dead man.

F.M. stepped over and said, "You all right, Eutychus?"

He didn't answer her. He just continued to stare down at the dead body.

"All right, you Tillmen men get on back to your cow camp," ordered Jubal. He knew they had set up camp a mile out of Waco.

"Mr. Tillman ain't going to like this, Marshal," said one of the men as he gripped his whiskey glass and slowly drank down the contents. Slamming down the glass on the counter, he wiped his mouth, burped, and cast a vicious stare at Jubal. Then he waved to the men and they moved toward the door.

F.M. continued holding her pistol, watching the drovers one by one as they left. It wouldn't be the first time a drunken cowboy tried his luck with his pistol as he was exiting.

The only man now left at the bar was Snake Jeffers. Jubal had seen him when he first came through the back door.

"All right, Jeffers, you ready to try and collect your wages?"

Jeffers chuckled. Eutychus couldn't believe anybody who had just seen Stone draw on Tadlock would have the courage to brace him. But Snake just chuckled and answered, "Not yet, Stone. Not yet." Then he pointed at Jubal and shook his finger. "But I'll let you know."

As Jeffers walked by Eutychus, he stopped and looked him up and down. "When I get shut of the marshal, you're next."

To everybody's surprise, Bly slapped Jeffers and said, "How about now?" Eutychus dropped his pistol back into leather and stared into Snake's eyes.

"You're mighty anxious to die, aren't you, mister?" asked Jeffers calmly. "But I wouldn't get paid to kill *you*."

Eutychus Bly looked like a man possessed. It was if something had come over him, just like it did with Jubal when he was dealing with killers like Jeffers.

"You threaten the marshal's life, it's the same as you threaten me or any other lawman in Waco."

F.M. started to say something to calm Eutychus down but Jubal waved her off with his eyes. The marshal knew this was an appointed time for Eutychus. He was finding his feet. Stone, however, kind of wished it wasn't a gunman of Jeffers' status, but that couldn't be helped.

"Nah... I believe I'll just get me a bottle and mosey on out of town. But you and me will meet up soon enough. What's your name, mister?"

"I'm done talking to you. Now get," said Eutychus, his hand positioned less than an inch from his gun.

Jeffers flipped a dollar on the bar and grabbed up the bottle the barkeep overheard him say he wanted. Then he walked slowly to the door. Looking over his shoulder, he said, "This night ain't over, Stone. See you directly."

Jeffers ran smack into Curly's chest. Then he turned around at the marshal's words.

"You better hope not, Snake. I see you again, it'll be down the barrel of my Colt."

Jeffers stepped around the frowning blacksmith, gripping the Winchester, and climbed down the steps. Pushing the bottle of whiskey into his saddlebags, he unhitched his horse and rode out of town.

Curly watched him disappear then stepped inside the saloon.

Four men had already hauled Tadlock off to the doc and two more men were toting out the dead man Eutychus had killed.

Jubal stared at his three deputies and said, "I could use a shot of rye... over at the office. How about you, Eutychus?"

"I ain't a drinking man, Marshal, but right about now, I figure I need a swallow of courage."

"Not from what I just saw you don't." Jubal patted Bly on the shoulder as they walked to the door. "You've got the hair of the bear. I believe you're going to do just fine in Kansas."

As they started out the door, Jubal turned to the saloon owner. "Barclay, you know what to do."

"Right, Marshal."

F.M. looked to Barclay then back to Jubal. She didn't know that the marshal had devised a plan to keep Tillman and his men from treeing the town. Across the street in just a few minutes, she would.

As they entered the jail, Jubal walked straight to his desk and opened the bottom drawer. Pulling out new bottle of rye that Judge Brewster had given him, he motioned for Curly to grab four glasses on the shelf by the coffee pot.

Pouring two fingers into each glass, Jubal set down the bottle and said, "May we all live till morning."

"Hear, hear," F.M. said, then they raised their glasses and drank down the liquor. When she put hers down, she cleared her throat and said, "All right, Jubal, what do you have up your sleeve? I heard what you said to Barclay."

"Figured you did, F.M.," grinned Jubal. "About now, six riflemen are getting positioned on the rooftops. They've been instructed to stay there until morning. I've given them orders to shoot anybody destroying property or causing harm to any citizen. I figure Tillman is going to send his men into town three or four at a time through the night. Then in the morning, we'll see Jeffers again, just as Tillman and his men are loading the cattle. He'll call me out."

"Waiting is bad for us and good for them, Marshal," said Curly. "I've heard you say that many times."

Jubal smiled across the room at the blacksmith. "You're right, Deputy Snipes. That's why we're going to pay Tillman and his men a visit in their camp outside of town. But first, we're going down to the corral and take a gander at them brands. I thought about waiting until morning, but like you said, Curly, waiting is good for them and bad for us."

"I'll fetch some lanterns," said F.M.

"I'll help you," said Curly.

Jubal smiled and said, "Yeah, Curly, you help Miller with those lanterns."

F.M. tossed him a vicious smile then waved Curly forward.

Eutychus stared at the door not saying a word. Jubal was a little concerned about him.

"You all right, Deputy Bly?"

"Ain't so sure, Marshal. I killed a man tonight. Don't reckon I'll be forgetting that for a long time."

"Well, I hope you don't, Eutychus. If killing ever becomes easy to you, you done lost your soul. The Good Lord put a reverence in our hearts for lives, but sometimes to protect one, you have to take one. Tonight was one of those times."

"Something came over me that I don't rightly understand. It just took hold of me and before I knew it, I shot that man."

"That same thing happens to me, Eutychus. I can't say that I understand it, but I believe it heightens my senses, quickens my draw, and helps me make split-second decisions that I figure has saved my life many times."

"Reckon what it is, Marshal?"

"Don't know, but the times it's happened was when I was dealing with men who had no respect for the lives of others. No respect for law. Maybe it's what the preachers call a righteous indignation."

Jubal heard F.M. and Snipes coming with the lanterns. They checked them for fuel and topped off the two that were low.

Stone reached in his pocket for a match as Curly was raising the chimneys. Soon all four lanterns were burning brightly.

"I sent word to Henry to have some fellows meet us at the pens. They'll be familiar with Tillman's brand. I figure we'll find a few doctored ones soon enough. Then we'll hightail it to Tillman's cowboy camp and pay him a visit."

It didn't take the lawmen long with the help of the train employees to find suspicious brands on forty-six head of steers. Several of Tillman's men attempted to head for camp to warn their boss, but Jubal stopped them. In fact, he locked them up and had Curly guard them with his Winchester.

With evidence now in hand, Jubal rounded up Miller and Bly and they rode for Tillman's camp. When they got within three hundred yards of it, they tied off their horses and snaked their way closer. Just thirty yards away, they ducked down behind some brush and heard an interesting conversation taking place between Tillman and Jeffers around the fire.

"Two hours from now, we're going to set Waco on fire. I want you to call out that marshal and gun 'im. I ain't right sure why you didn't do it earlier in the saloon."

"I done told you, Tillman. One of his deputies had the jump on me. He'd done killed one of your men. To boot, Stone was standing off to my right. Now what was I supposed to do? Get myself kilt?"

Jubal counted twenty-two men milling about the camp. Some of them had their own fires burning and were drinking coffee and whiskey and playing cards.

Whispering, Jubal said, "I figure I can slip right in there to where Tillman and Jeffers are without getting them others stirred up. I'm going to circle around and ease into the camp from yonder direction like I was one of Tillman's men. Then I'll move toward those two idiots and try to persuade them to come without a fight."

"All right, Jubal. We'll stay put and cover you. Holler if you need us, and we'll come running," whispered Miller.

Eutychus pointed to the tree line. "Marshal, there's a fellow standing over there in the shadows with a rifle in his hand. You go that way, and you'll run smack into him."

Jubal squinted and studied where Eutychus pointed but couldn't see anything. F.M. did the same thing. Suddenly they saw the strike of a match. The man's face lit up for just a second before he put the flame to his cigarette.

Stone shook his head. "Glad you saw him, Eutychus. I blame sure didn't."

F.M. chuckled softly. "Mr. Bly's got the vision of a night owl."

Jubal went in from another direction and soon stepped right up behind Tillman and Jeffers, arresting them both. Neither gave the marshal any trouble. Of course, it was probably because the promise he made to both of them as he thumbed back his hammer and disarmed them.

"Tillman, when I tell you, get up and walk toward my two deputies that have their guns trained on you right now. They're about thirty yards yonder way. You yell out and they'll pump your gut full of lead."

Jubal looked around, watching the cowboys mingling about. They didn't seem to suspect anything. "Now, Tillman, move," ordered Jubal.

"Didn't figure you to be yeller, Stone," said Jeffers softly. "Heard you were the type that faced a man head on. Reckon I heard wrong, you sneaking in here like you did."

Jubal smiled. "Jeffers, taking you and Tillman were as easy as taking candy from a baby. You gun slicks are a dumb lot. Get moving." He shook his pistol in the direction Claude had walked.

When Jubal reached Miller and Bly, they had Tillman in hand irons and aboard Razor, F.M.'s gelding.

"Put the irons on Jeffers and let's hoist him up behind Tillman. Miller, you best ride with me. Ain't sure if Bly's roan doubles yet."

Jubal and his deputies rode into Waco and went straight to the jail. When they got the two men locked into cells, the four lawmen stepped outside on the stoop. The cells were beginning to fill up. Jubal sat down on the bench and waved at the man on the rooftop of the building across the street. In another hour, it would be light.

"Curly, you go down to that end of town. F.M., you and Eutychus take that end. I'm going to sit tight. Figure Tillman's men will be riding in here shortly. I plan to arrest every one of them we can. As far as I'm concerned, if they work for Claude, they're cattle rustlers."

Over twenty men rode up to the jail, asking if Stone knew where their boss was.

Jubal threw a thumb over his shoulder. "Yep. He's in there. Now, you boys drop your guns and climb down off those animals. You're all under arrest for cattle rustling. And before you do something stupid and pull those hawglegs, the rooftops are full of Winchesters."

F.M. and Eutychus rushed up behind the cowboys with drawn guns. Each man slowly dropped his pistol into the dirt and climbed down. All except two—Bart Evans, Tillman's foreman, and Latigo, the gunman Jubal had come across down at the stockyard earlier.

"Nobody takes my gun," said Latigo as he looked over his shoulder at the deputies then back in front of him to Jubal.

Eutychus' blood began to boil. He bolted toward Latigo and pulled him down off his horse. Jubal snatched iron and stepped toward Bart.

"Step down while you can, mister. I won't tell you again," demanded Jubal.

Bart did as he was told. There were just too many guns pointed at him to do otherwise.

F.M. stepped up closer to Eutychus who had tied up with Latigo. Latigo got to his feet and punched Bly in the belly, but before he could hit him again, Eutychus caught him with an uppercut to the chin. Latigo went for his gun, which was laying a few feet away. F.M. started for hers when Jubal called her off.

Eutychus pulled Latigo by the legs back away from the pistol. Then he flipped him over and pounded him with his fist. Rolling him back over, he looked to F.M., motioning for a pair of hand irons. She tossed them his way and watched him put them on Latigo. Pulling him to his feet, he grabbed him by the arm toward the jail.

Jubal motioned for Bart to follow, and he did.

That night in Waco, Eutychus Bly came into his own. He proved he had the mettle to be a lawman. Over the next three months, he continued to serve as one of Jubal Stone's deputies, even after Tanner Burns returned from Burnett.

Eutychus Bly and his family ended up spending eight months in Waco. The townsfolk had grown to love them. They were good people, hard workers, and the kind of folks any town would appreciate having. But it was time for them to head back to Kansas.

Marshal Stone and Deputy Miller had taught Eutychus everything they could about being a lawman in the time they had, and he had proved to them that he was a good student. Now, it was time for him to ride the Kansas Plains and do the job Governor Hoppe had commissioned him to do.

The night before they would board the train out of Waco, the judge, along with the Stones, Curly Snipes, Tanner Burns, and F.M. Miller threw them a going away party at one of the diners in Waco.

As the party was ending, Jubal stepped over to Del and handed him a brand new Winchester. Nancy gave Myra and quilt she and Lucy Brewster had sewed, and F.M. gave Eutychus a pair of binoculars, even though she said with his vision he didn't really need them.

All three of the Blys were in tears over the generosity they'd been shown. When they arrived in Waco eight months previously, they were a dispirited family that had just about lost all hope. Now, they were ready to get back to Kansas and start a new chapter in their lives.

As they said their goodbyes the next morning, Myra and Nancy hugged. Jubal shook Del's hand and said, "It's been a pleasure meeting you, son. You take care of your ma and pa."

"I will, Marshal, and I won't never forget you as long as I live."

Del grabbed Jubal around the waist. Wiping tears from his own eyes, Jubal patted him on the head. "You're a good man, Del Bly. Maybe one day soon we'll come see you in Kansas."

Del nodded and looked away.

Jubal stepped over to Eutychus. "If you ever need me or Deputy Miller for anything, you let us know and we'll jump a train and be on our way." Jubal had no idea when he made that offer that soon he would be enroute to Kansas to help the Blys.

"Obliged, Jubal, for all you did for me." Eutychus looked around. "I wanted to say goodbye to F.M. but I reckon she's..."

"Yeah, I've got her serving a warrant this morning. Besides, she's not much on goodbyes."

"All aboard," yelled the conductor.

Eutychus helped Myra up the steps. Del was right behind her. Eutychus stepped up on the stairs and waved. "We'll write you soon and let you know where we light."

"Take care, Eutychus," said Jubal as he put his arm around Nancy who was holding Monty, then the train pulled away.

"And don't forget Blue in the livery car. He'll need water at your next stop."

A month later, Jubal Stone received a disturbing telegram from Myra Bly. In it, Mrs. Bly said that Del had been injured and Eutychus needed help. "Your help would be appreciated, even though Eutychus would never ask for it," she wrote.

As Jubal stared down at the telegram, many thoughts ran through his head. *Did I do Eutychus an injustice by training him to be a lawman? Should I have insisted he stay a farmer? What kind of injury does Del have? Does it have anything to do with Eutychus being a range detective?*

Jubal's hands balled into fists. He slammed them both down on the desk as F.M. walked in. She knew something was wrong by the look on Jubal's face. As she closed the door behind her, she mustered the courage to ask.

"What's the matter, Jubal?"

He grabbed up the telegram and spun it on his desk. She stepped over and picked it up. As she read it, she gasped. Then, she too began to wonder if they had done right by the Blys.

"When do we leave, Jubal? And this time, there ain't nothing that's going to keep me in Waco. I'm going, even if you don't."

Jubal sighed. "Figure to go have a talk with the judge." He walked swiftly toward the door. Then he spun on his heels. "Get packed, F.M. We're headed to Kingman, Kansas."

If you enjoyed this Western adventure, be sure to check out Susan Payne's *Midwest Mail Order Brides* series! CLICK HERE to get your copy of book one, *Montana Lineman.*

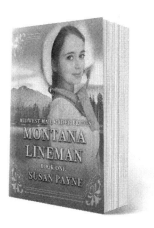

Vince wanted a family, a friend, and a lover. Daisy desired the same. Could the two young people make a lasting marriage when neither knew how to be what the other needed? One knew what a family should be, the other only thought he knew. Could Vince save his marriage after his disastrous mistakes in the beginning? And would Daisy find peace with her choice?

The adventure continues with Susan Payne's *Texas Rangers Romance* series! CLICK HERE to get your copy of book one, *In The Sheriff's Sights.*

Texas Ranger Crocker loves being a lawman and is fascinated with the female sheriff. Jessie Heinz loves being a sheriff but wants more for herself. Should the combustible couple allow sparks to fly? Or call it quits to preserve the peace?

Printed in Great Britain
by Amazon

17079431R00084